RADIUM GIRL

RADIUM GIRL

stories

SOFI PAPAMARKO

A Buckrider Book

Buckrider Books is an imprint of Wolsak and Wynn Publishers.

Editor for Buckrider Books: Paul Vermeersch | Editor: Jen Sookfong Lee | Copy editor: Ashley Hisson
Cover and interior design: Michel Vrana
Cover image: iStockphoto.com
Author photograph: Jennifer Rowsom
Typeset in Sabon and Break Loose
Printed by Rapido Books, Montreal, Canada
Printed on certified 100% post-consumer Rolland Enviro Paper.

Lyrics from Honest Ed's store song reproduced with permission from Mirvish Productions.

10 9 8 7 6 5 4 3 2 1

The publisher gratefully acknowledges the support of the Toronto Arts Council, the Ontario Arts Council, the Canada Council for the Arts and the Government of Canada.

Buckrider Books
280 James Street North
Hamilton, ON
Canada L8R 2L3

Library and Archives Canada Cataloguing in Publication
Title: Radium girl : stories / Sofi Papamarko.
Names: Papamarko, Sofi, 1980- author.
Identifiers: Canadiana 20200410660 | ISBN 9781989496268 (softcover)
Subjects: LCGFT: Short stories.
Classification: LCC PS8631.A63 R33 2021 | DDC C813/.6—dc23

Table of Contents

Margie & Lu / 1

The Pollinators / 27

Everyone You Love Is Dead / 35

White Cake / 49

Tiny Girls / 69

Controlled Burn / 81

Ark / 97

Something to Cry About / 105

Underwater Calisthenics / 131

In Heaven, Everything Is Fine / 141

Five Full-Colour Dreams of a Young Marie Curie / 151

Radium Girl / 159

Acknowledgements / 173

Notes / 175

Margie & Lu

Lu

We were born the day the *Challenger* space shuttle exploded. Things have only gone downhill from there.

I don't say *I* because we are unequivocally a *we*. We have always been a *we* and we always will be. My twin sister and I took our first breaths seconds apart. We've been told we'll die minutes apart. And we'll do absolutely everything together, all of that time in between.

My sister's name is Margaret. She also goes by Margie or Marg, if you want to save yourself a couple of syllables. We're very close, Margie and me. You might even say we're attached at the hip.

That's not technically true. We have two hips, just like you. Two hips, two legs, two feet, ten toes. It's above the waist where things get a little more complicated. Surgeons tell us we have four lungs – albeit one of mine is slightly underdeveloped and leaves me wheezy on hot, humid days. Two spines. Two hearts. One shared digestive tract, snaking its way through both of our torsos. We share most vital and reproductive organs, actually. So no, we're not attached at the hip, clever as that idiom may be in our case. We're attached at the chest cavity. *Dicephalic*

1

parapagus twins. We're conjoined twins, using the most basic terminology.

My name is Luna. Our mother says I was named after Lunenburg, Nova Scotia, where she went on a high school trip once, but I like to tell people I was named for the moon. It fits. If Margie is the sun, I am her pale reflection. Her shadow. People get pulled into Margie's glorious, gregarious orbit every single day. I am the only one who has no choice in the matter.

Our internal wiring is too intertwined for us to ever be separated; we will never lead separate lives. I've long given up hope that we ever will. But not a day goes by when I don't wish things were profoundly different. Margie, on the other hand, doesn't seem to mind our lot in life one bit. She actually enjoys all of the fuss and attention of being my very close neighbour. She knows it makes her extra special. She knows it makes her worthier of attention.

I don't go for attention. I'm not fond of fuss. All I want is a little peace and quiet. Is that too much to ask? All I want is a seat in a plush library with shelves upon shelves of leather-bound first editions that smell like paper and rot and the passage of time and the gift of perfect, expansive silence. Silence so vast and encompassing, it's practically a solid object.

Would you laugh at me if I told you that loneliness is a luxury?

Margie

Some people spend their whole lives trying to get famous. My sister and I, we were *born* famous.

The Saint John *Telegraph-Journal* was the first coverage we got. "Rare Conjoined Twin Girls Born in Bathurst." There's a photo of us in an incubator, all veiny and purple, with the little yellow hats and booties Mum knitted for us while she was pregnant. We were front-page news and the talk of New Brunswick! We'd have been the biggest news story of the day, too, if that stupid space shuttle hadn't exploded.

It only took a day or two before my sister and I became world-famous. The *Washington Post*, the *New York Times*, the *Guardian*. They all wrote about us. All of them! They still do, sometimes, on our birthday. Mum saves all of our newspaper and magazine clippings in a giant scrapbook. We still take it out and read the clips sometimes.

There was this piece that came out in the *Toronto Star* not long after our tenth birthday that I really like. It was a couple of years after Mum moved us to Toronto permanently to be closer to the very best doctors in the country, not to mention all of the university hospitals that wanted to study us. We ended up moving into an apartment on Bathurst Street in Toronto, which I think our mum did on purpose to help us feel less homesick. We would still be the Bathurst twins! Anyway, I like to read this one section of the article out loud over and over and over until Luna gets pissed off and tells me to give it a rest:

The Bathurst Twins, despite sharing corporeal real estate, are two very distinct young ladies. Margie (Margaret) Provencher is an enchanting creature – lovely and wild, wilful and loud. This ebullient extrovert, head piled high with chestnut curls reminiscent of a young Mary Pickford, loves to sing, dance and mug for the camera. Her delicate upturned nose lends an air of aristocracy, despite the fact that the twins were born to a single mother in rural New Brunswick. Indeed, one can't help but think that bedimpled little Margie could have starred in commercials or even made it big in Hollywood had the circumstances of her birth and life been different. It's impossible not to be charmed by this pretty little dynamo.

Luna is the shy one. Quiet and introspective, her forte is language. Both girls are fluently bilingual, but Lu has already taught herself Latin and is presently dabbling in Italian, Spanish and Mandarin. I ask her to conjugate Latin verbs for me. She does so effortlessly and in a tone that announces her utter boredom. Lu is moon-faced and her skull is slightly misshapen. Looking at her is like looking at the lovely Margie's reflection in a funhouse mirror. She probably has much to say, but allows her sister to do most of the talking.

Lu

I hate that article. Hated that interview, too. That reporter was about a hundred years old, kept touching us on the arms and thighs and leaned in to kiss us at the end – like holy shit! Landed square on Margie's lips, the sad old pervert. I turned my head away, but I knew it wasn't my lips he wanted. His beard was yellow and his nails were too and he smelled like he'd been marinating in Scotch and old cigarette butts for decades.

Margie

There's a photo of us, too. We're blowing out the candles on our birthday cake (Black Forest cake from Safeway, my favourite, I really do remember it). My eyes are wide and dark. Luna's cheeks are all puffed out and her eyes are scrunched shut. We're both wearing polka-dotted paper party hats with those pinching elastic strings around our chins. There are a few headless people in the background wearing hospital scrubs. Mum's on the far left, saying something frozen in time.

I remember exactly what I wished for. Every year, when I blow out the candles on our birthday cake, I wish for the exact same thing. I want a boyfriend. I've wanted a boyfriend since I was like six and I wish for one every year. I wonder how many birthdays it will take? How many candles? How many flames do I have to extinguish before I finally get to fall in love? I've never even kissed a boy before and I'm already so old.

Below the photo, in italics: *"Margaret and Luna Provencher celebrate their tenth birthday at Sick Kids Hospital, surrounded by their medical team."*

I don't know what Luna wished for on that birthday or any birthday. We never tell each other what we wish for. If we did, our wishes might never come true.

Lu

I've read everything I can get my hands on about our – look, I really hesitate to call it a condition. Our *situation*, let's say. *Condition* makes it sound like we're old and frail and piss ourselves every hour. It's nothing like that. We're young and strong and healthy. We're capable and mostly independent. We're only seventeen.

Two years before we were born, an article about conjoined twins was published in a medical journal. I found a microfiche in the Toronto Reference Library when I was supposed to be doing another research project. One line from that article has stuck with me ever since: "Two people never being able to obtain privacy – to bathe, excrete, copulate, or eat – defies imagination."

I found the sentiment . . . odd. Margie and I are different people, sure, but we share this body. Why should we be shy about bathing or taking a shit? It's *our* body! Are you embarrassed taking a bath alone with your own body? Do you feel strange peeing while you're in the same room as your body? No? Well, same.

Eating, too, is a breeze. We take turns these days for the sake of efficiency and also, in the words of Margie, to watch our waistline. Margie lets me have breakfast, because I love oatmeal with fruit and I can enjoy a leisurely cup of coffee while I read the *Globe and Mail*. Margie takes lunch, which is fine by me – I read philosophy tomes while she mows down on a sandwich and apple and chats with her friends in the cafeteria. At dinnertime, we alternate and negotiate, depending on what Mum has prepared. Margie takes one for the team whenever pork is involved. Brussels sprouts and peas are all mine. Lasagna night? We take turns. For both ethical and environmental reasons, I have seriously been considering veganism. Margie rolls her eyes and says, "That'll sure be fun!"

Copulate.

Margie is convinced she's going to meet someone. She's dreamt up a magical, understanding prince of a man who will fall in love with both of us at the same time. One wedding, two sets of vows. "That would be awfully convenient," I say. "He'd be living the dream! Threesomes every night!"

Margie tells me to shut my idiot mouth. She doesn't see me pull a face because we aren't able to directly look at each other, except when we're looking into a mirror. I try to avoid my own reflection but steal glances at Margie in the mirror whenever I can, if I'm being perfectly honest.

My sister is very beautiful. It's the second thing people notice about her.

Margie

Can I tell you about a dream I had last night?

I'm in the middle of a huge athletic arena. The seats are all empty, but the lights are on. Including a heavy-duty spotlight pointed right at me. I'm wearing a silver sequined leotard and am powdering my hands with chalk dust. I'm practising a gymnastics routine and it's a big deal. Like, *a very big deal*. And I am under a *lot* of pressure. It's not like any routine you've ever seen on TV for the Olympics. It's a lot longer and more complicated than that.

The arena is quiet because it's completely empty. I'm the only one there.

I start out on the uneven bars and flip myself around like it's nothing. Like I'm in an antigravity chamber or something. I am practically weightless, and pin-straight. I fly off the bars to land effortlessly on the balance beam. I backflip my way across it, nailing the landings every single time. From there, I leap directly to the rings and hold my body parallel to the floor for what seems like eons. I'm not even shaking – that's how strong and solid I am. Finally, I dismount and twist and cartwheel across the floor, leaving a trail of flames behind me. I do a little curtsy to the empty stands but an audience has appeared. It's a full house. Everyone erupts into cheers and I get a standing ovation. I see my mum in the front row. She's crying. Dozens of heavy-duty television cameras are pointed right at me. I can see my image projected on huge video screens around the arena. I wave and smile and my teeth are gleaming white like I'm a woman from a toothpaste ad. It's only when Lu runs over from the sidelines with an armful of red roses that I realize my sister hasn't been by my side the whole time. I had done something all by myself.

Lu

Mum demanded we start applying for summer jobs after we got our university acceptances, even though we both got full-ride scholarships at the University of Toronto to do a double major in Theatre (Margie's choice) and English Literature (mine). Mum really pushes for normalcy at every turn, which I can usually appreciate, but this time I was irritated with her. A full-time summer job left little time for pleasure reading and I had just discovered Nabokov.

After a resumé blitz in our neighbourhood, we were hired on as stock girls at Honest Ed's, which is this massive chintzy discount department store just a few blocks from our apartment. Honest Ed's is a living monument to tackiness: a Vegas-style marquee of a store taking up an entire square city block, plastered with slogans and cheeseball puns that I suppose might have been amusing in another era.

HONEST ED AIN'T UPPER CRUST! BUT HIS BARGAIN PRICES SAVE YOU DOUGH!!
HONEST ED'S A FREAK! HE HAS BARGAINS COMING OUT OF HIS EARS!!
ONLY THE FLOORS ARE CROOKED!!!
COME IN AND GET LOST!

We started off unpacking boxes from the loading dock, taking note of inventory and replenishing the shelves with canned goods and electric tape, jars of instant coffee and brightly coloured rubber balls that were Made in China. Our co-workers – all much older than us – marvelled at how seamlessly my sister and I worked together, like synchronized swimmers on dry land, pricing tinned tomatoes and marking down tubes of discontinued toothpaste.

It paid minimum wage and I found it boring as hell. Margie was thrilled, though. She couldn't stop gabbing about our new job to her friends over the phone, like going to work in that cheesy hellhole was some kind of glamorous accomplishment. As much as she revelled in being special, I knew there were times when she yearned to be just like everybody else.

Margie

When the store opened at 10:00 a.m., every single morning without fail, we played the Honest Ed's theme song over the intercom. It was this really goofy jingle written about a hundred years ago. The guy who sings it sounds like he's putting on a fake Jamaican accent. Luna says it's sexist and kind of racist because it was probably sung by a white guy and if that's the case, it's sort of making fun of the way Black people talk? I don't know. The words are a little bit ridiculous and the whole thing makes, like, zero sense, but I kind of like it. It's pretty funny. Sometimes I sing it in the shower really early, before our shift. One time, I got Lu to join in:

He sells pins and needles shoes and tacks
Shirts and ties and household wax
H-O-N-E-S-T E-D
Honest Ed's
Crazy Honest Ed's
How can he be honest when his prices are so low?
This guy chases a bargain like a woman would chase his dough
Now he's got a brand-new service
He'll sell you a wife tailor-made
And if you have a row with your mother-in-law
He'll take her back on a trade.

That weirdo song might be my second favourite thing about the store. My first favourite thing about Honest Ed's is how it's built like a kind of labyrinth. There are all sorts of weird storage rooms behind closed doors that are for staff use only. And since we're staff, we can explore and excavate them on our breaks. One of the secret rooms almost gave me a heart attack.

There's a white swinging door in the children's toy department with a painted sign on it that says AUTHORIZED PERSONNEL ONLY. Behind it, there's a series of ramps and hallways and conveyor belts that end up in the creepiest fucking room you've ever seen. We both screamed our heads off when we first went in there.

Lu

I thought we had innocently stumbled upon a mass murder scene, or maybe an open grave of people who had died from SARS. There were armless bodies and legless bodies, free-standing torsos and what looked like boxes of severed heads. Some of the mannequins were standing and some were lying down and some were sitting with their long legs crossed. They're all bald as chemo patients and garishly made-up – lipstick and eyeshadow like something out of an '80s music video. The mannequins are old – definitely way older than we are – so they're thick with dust and a lot of the flesh-coloured paint has been chipped away revealing putty grey underneath. Their eyes are unblinking and vacant and blue. There are mannequin arms grotesquely bent at the elbows and mannequin hands with nails the same colour as their flesh and dusty mannequin legs attached to beige stiletto heels. Many of the disembodied legs are all clustered together in one or two boxes. The toes point upwards, like alleyway flowers straining to seek out sunlight.

It's strange to me that mannequins are supposed to represent the ideal of womanhood when all mannequins look the same. Mannequins are never fat. Mannequins are usually white. Mannequins never ever have more than one head on their body. Mannequins never say a word.

Margie and I gravitate toward the mannequin room before and after our shifts to blow off some steam and be ridiculous.

"Alas, Poor Yorick!" Margie would say in her best overwrought actor voice, holding up a mannequin's torso holding its own head in its hand. "I knew him, Horatio. A fellow of infinite jest, of most excellent fancy . . ."

"Hey there, gorgeous. Would you like to dance?"

"I would, but I seriously have two left feet."

"That you do! Don't worry – I'll give you a . . . *hand*!"

By the end of our little plays, we would be in hysterics. We couldn't tear ourselves away from that place. But if I'm being honest with you, the mannequins – and that dark, hidden room – gave me a serious case of the creeps.

Margie

The store hired a couple of other new people halfway through the summer to help take on some shifts while the veteran workers took their vacations.

One of them is this girl Tracey who's around our age. Tracey's cool as hell. She always wears these long floral vintage dresses under her Honest Ed's shirts but never gets in trouble for violating the dress code because she's the manager's nephew's girlfriend. She's really pretty and has this super rad free-flowing bohemian style but she told us it's out of necessity because she's a fat girl and has trouble finding anything cute that fits. Tell me about it. Mum has to tailor most of our clothes.

The other new hire is this guy Alex Addorisio. We know him, of course. Or at least, we know of him. He was in our grade. We'd just never really talked to him or gotten to know him at school at all. We were never in any of the same classes. Alex was on the rugby team last year. He's Irish-Italian and he likes to joke that his favourite food is spaghetti with Lucky Charms sprinkled on top. That made me laugh. He's a little on the short side but pretty handsome, really. All the girls at school super thought so, too.

Lu

Alex is a genuine turd and dumber than any mannequin. He repeats that Lucky Charms joke literally every day. He uses words like *Paki* and *retard* and *gypped* on a daily basis and addresses everyone as "Hey, guy!" instead of bothering to learn their actual names. Otherwise, he mostly expresses himself in grunts, monosyllables and jokes about blondes and Newfies. Naturally, Margie hasn't stopped talking about him.

Margie

Tracey throws a party every Labour Day weekend. She hand-delivered our invitations at work. She said her parents would be at her grandparents' cottage in Haliburton this year, so we'd have the entire house to ourselves.

"No parents, no rules, no bullshit," she said. "My boyfriend and his college friends will buy enough booze to go around, but make sure you bring ten bucks to contribute to the cause."

On the back of the invitation, it said, "Destroy with fire after memorizing address." This party was a secret. This party was all ours.

Lu

I didn't really want to go to the party, but I genuinely liked Tracey and didn't want to be seen as completely anti-social. Plus, I wouldn't want to take the experience away from Margie. Sometimes I have to take one for the team. I wasn't going to have fun but, I mean, it would be fine. *Carpe diem* and all of that.

The thing was, we were scheduled to work an opening shift at the store early the next morning. Margie promised we wouldn't stay at the party too late.

Margie

Tracey lives in this old Victorian row house not far from our place. It's like something out of a movie, I swear! Stained glass, pine floors, an ancient brick fireplace, the works. We told Mum Tracey's parents would be chaperoning. Plus, we had our new flip phones and would text if we needed to get in touch with her.

At Lu's insistence, we leave right at 8:00 p.m. We are the very first guests to arrive, which is slightly humiliating, but Tracey seems genuinely happy to see us. She gives us a tour that ends in the kitchen, where there's a row of unopened booze lining the counter – brown and green and crystal clear bottles.

Aside from having a few sips of wine at a family friend's wedding last year, Luna and I have never actually had any alcohol before. But I'm not about to tell that to anyone. Least of all Tracey, who is beyond cool.

"I was hoping they were going to get more hard stuff than that," Tracey sighs. "Don't worry – the kegs are being delivered in like half an hour."

We meet Tracey's boyfriend, Tim. He is really nice, just like Tracey. But then his buddies start showing up. They all go to the same suburban college and walk around in clouds of cheap cologne. Every single one of them seems to own a Honda Civic. They're parked up and down the street. One of them is blasting a remix of 50 Cent's "In Da Club" from his car stereo and it's battling with the house party music, which right now is shuffling between a Wilco CD and Sleater-Kinney.

Lu

"Well, I'll be good goddamned!" says one of Tracey's boyfriend's friends, grinning menacingly at us. "A bitch with two heads!"

A flash of red. I'm stunned. Enraged. Gut-churningly humiliated. We forget sometimes. We're so used to our school friends and our colleagues treating us with dignity and respect and like human beings that we forget we're different. Different enough that certain people think we should be treated as less than human. They see us as circus freaks, sideshow fodder, *monsters*.

"My name is Margaret, how very lovely to make your acquaintance," says Margie, poised and charming. She reaches out her pale slender hand, gingerly latching onto his red meaty one. "This is my twin sister, Luna. We're going to the University of Toronto in the fall on a full scholarship. How about yourself?" The friend, suddenly sheepish, mutters, "Nice meeting you," and retreats to the backyard.

Game, set, match.

"Let's get ourselves a fucking drink," says my sister.

Margie

That prick that prick that fucking prick fuck that fucking prick fuck that prick fuck him

I'm yelling. I might be crying. We're in the basement. Alex is holding my face and telling me to calm down. I tell him what happened and he's telling me that it's okay, it's okay. That Tracey's boyfriend's friends are just a bunch of frat boy douches. He tells me that I'm beautiful.

"You do know that, don't you, Margie? You're gorgeous. Seriously hot, okay?" He looks me in the eye for a few seconds. And then he goes outside for a smoke.

When he comes back, he unzips his backpack and waves a silver bottle in the air.

"I stole the good tequila," Alex says. "Let's do shots, ladies!"

Lu

We're pretty drunk, Margie. I think you need to take it easy now. We're not used to this.

Margie

Whatever, *Mom.*

Lu

I don't know what time it is. The party is winding down. Soon it will be time to leave. Thank god. Thank god. My head hurts. Alex is whispering things into Margie's ear. Margie is laughing this insanely high-pitched laugh. She sounds like a hyena after huffing from a helium balloon. I've never, ever heard her laugh like that.

There are only six or seven of us left here. The college bros are long gone. Tracey reamed them out when she caught three of them smoking weed in one of the bedrooms.

"No smoking inside, dumbasses!" Tracey shrieked. "You want me to catch serious shit from my folks?"

"This party sucks," said one of the bros as he left. "High school girls are so uptight."

I want to go now.

I want to go.

Can we *please* go now?

Margie

Fine. We can go. Let's go!

Lu

Relief washes over me . . . until I realize Alex is coming with us. And where we're going is not home.

Margie

We are standing beneath the marquee of Honest Ed's. It's gone dark now, but the streetlights and moonlight are bright enough that we can see everything.

Honest Ed's a freak! He has prices coming out of his ears!

A freak. A freak. That *word*. Applied to me. Applied to us.

Our stomach lurches. We will never be free of this. We'll go to university and people in our classes will stare at us, pass notes to each other, look away in discomfort or disgust. Professors won't know who to look at when they call on us. Boys will date our friends but not us. Never us. Why date a freak when you can date someone normal? Only freaks date freaks.

But here we are with Alex. He's looking at me in a way that makes me feel good and weird at the same time. I want him to keep looking at me, but I also want him to stop staring. Staring doesn't feel good to people like us. I look up and away and he does the same.

"You know, I've never noticed all of this writing, like, all of these funny signs and stuff," says Alex. "It's pretty cool. It reminds me of the olden days or something."

I can hear Lu exhale sharply. I can sense her thinking, "God, what an idiot."

"It says 'Once in a lifetime,'" says Alex. Now he is staring at me again. I can smell the tequila on his breath and see the wanting in his eyes. Oh my god. Alex wants me. *Someone wants me.*

Just close your eyes, Lu, if you're tired. Like all those nights you wanted to stay up and read and I didn't. Like those nights when I took improv classes and you didn't even want to be there. Close your eyes, Sister, I'll take it from here. I've already texted Mum that we're sleeping over at Tracey's. That's just a teeny tiny white lie because we'll just be in another safe place. A place we know very well.

I promised you we wouldn't be late for opening shift, remember? Well, guess what, Sis? We're five hours early for work. Isn't that something?

Lu

We enter the store through the alleyway. Margie and Alex have thrown on all of the fluorescents and I get hit with a sensation like red-hot nails being hammered into my eyeballs. Is it possible we've only been drunk for a few hours and I'm already suffering from a hangover? Alex has his arm around our waist.

"Have you seen the mannequin room yet?"

"The what?"

(Goddamnit, she's going to show that moron our secret place. But it's *ours*.)

We lead him to the toy department. Well, Margie does. I just follow the neural instructions she drops like bread crumbs for me to follow. Left foot. Right foot. Through the DO NOT ENTER door. Onto the ramp. Into the mannequin room.

COME IN AND GET LOST!

It smells strangely different here at night. The corners look darker. I shiver from the cold and from something else. Fear, I think. Disgust, maybe. I want to go home.

"This room is fucking rad, I can't believe I didn't know about it before!" Alex wolf-whistles. "Look at all them pretty titties." He presses his body against an armless mannequin and feigns licking her breast before plucking off her plastic head and lobbing it at us. Lobbing it at me. Hard.

"What the hell, dude?" I say.

"*Chill, guy,*" says Alex. "Geez, I thought chicks loved it when you gave them head." Margie laughs her hysterical, ridiculous hyena laugh.

"That was shitty, Alex," I tell him. "That *hurt.*"

He shrugs. I continue to glare him down.

Then, "I guess you don't need another head."

He picks up a mannequin leg and caresses it. Runs his tongue up and down the thigh. Slowly dry humps a free-standing torso and moans loudly in faux pleasure while making a goofy, contorted face. God, I hate him.

"I'm the only man in an entire room of beautiful, naked women," says Alex. "I have got to say, this is truly the dream. Truly every man's dream."

Then he looks me and my sister up and down and says, "Why are you still dressed?"

Margie

I feel his lips on my mouth. Warm and soft and inviting. A little bristly around the chin. His tongue slides into my mouth like a hot slug. I can't believe this is happening. I can't believe this is happening with Alex! No more dress rehearsals. No more practise kissing my pillow at night. This is real. My life – my actual real life – is finally beginning.

Lu

Shit.

Margie

There's a little side room. Just off the mannequin room. It's mostly for storage. Usually, it's full of blue and yellow shopping bags and brackets and shelves waiting to be filled. It's empty tonight, with the exception of the two of us. Well, the three of us. The floor is old splintering wood but it's okay. It might hurt us tomorrow. It might hurt tonight. But everything hurts all the time, so why not the good things, too? Why not the best things in life?

Lu

I don't want to. I don't want it. Margie. Margie, we haven't even talked about this! Margie, I'm right here! You don't get to decide this on your own. You don't get to decide this in the moment without a conversation. You don't get to decide this while we're still so drunk.

"You're so beautiful, baby," Alex says. "Yeah, you like that?"

"No. Alex," I say. "Stop. Alex, please!"

"Quiet, *freak*," Alex whispers menacingly in my ear. Margie pretends she doesn't hear. Margie is somewhere else now. But I am still right here.

Margie

Neither of us chose this body. We didn't choose this life. Why can't I have what I want, just this once?

Lu

Sometimes I wonder if we would even be friends if we hadn't been sisters. I love you, Margie, but I don't think we ever would have been. In moments like this, you feel like a stranger.

Margie

Let me have this. Please. Just let me have this.

Lu

You can! You will! When it's right. When we're agreed. I promise you will. But for right now, I need you to make him stop.

Margie

What if this is my only chance? We're *freaks*, remember?

Lu

ego sum

tu es

is/ea/id est

nos sumus

vos estis

ei/eae/ea sunt

COME IN AND GET LOST!

COME IN AND GET LOST!

COME IN AND GET LOST!

COME IN AND GET LOST!

COME IN AND GET LOST!

COME IN AND GET LOST!

Margie

Just close your eyes, dear sister. From everything I've ever heard, it'll be over so fast.

Lu

A fellow came over from England
As he went down Bloor Street way
He saw a sign that read Buckingham Palace
H-E is in today
So he went upstairs
And he knocked on the door
And a fellow came out and said
"H-E" doesn't mean Her Excellency
It stands for Honest Ed's
He sells pins and needles, shoes and tacks
Shirts and ties and household wax
H-O-N-E-S-T E-D
Honest Ed's
Crazy Honest Ed's

What I said before about loneliness? I was wrong. It's not a privilege. And it's something you can definitely still be, even when you're around other people. Especially when you're around other people. Loneliness is an art form and I think my sister and I may have just perfected it.

*

Nos sumus: we are. Always we, never me. Together forever, sweet Sister. Locked in. One.

Nos sumus: we are.

Ego sum: I am.

I am.

I am.

I am.

I am here.

I am still right here.

The Pollinators

THE WORLD CAN END IN SO MANY WAYS.

Pathogens locked up in Arctic permafrost for millennia are slowly waking up – an army of single-celled Rip Van Winkles. As the north continues to warm and thaw, zombie bacteria and previously unknown viruses will be released into the world like the contents of some terrifying new Pandora's box. The illnesses would spread quickly, thanks to intercontinental travel. Not everyone on earth would die, of course, but civilization would collapse like dominoes. Cities would be abandoned. Life, as we know it, would end. Gamma ray bursts from the sun are my greatest hope for us, really. It would be blessedly quick. Not entirely clean, of course, but nothing that annihilates all sentient life on a planet ever could be. If you really think about it, a gamma ray burst is the brain aneurysm of doomsday scenarios. Instantaneous death. Painless, probably. We'd be dry-roasted like trussed-up Christmas turkeys in a nanosecond.

"Min," there is a note of warning in David's voice. "Let's talk about something else."

David's business partner Stuart and his wife, Camelia, are here. We are sitting in the dining room. Rich, dark mahogany. Candlelight. It's the nicest room in our house. We never use it.

27

"Gamma rays bursting, you say?" Stuart's eyebrow is raised. "What about the Rapture, eh? That would be something to behold. All of those naked, righteous souls floating like hot-air balloons to meet our Lord and Saviour. Quite the impressive mass exit!"

We are eating cashew chicken and jasmine rice with disposable chopsticks. This dish is the closest approximation of Chinese cooking I can muster. More North America's notion of Chinese cuisine, really, but I'm Vietnamese, so what the hell do I care? Whenever we entertain his colleagues and their partners, I know that David wants me to play up the role of Young Asian Wife, even though, at thirty-seven, I'm not specifically young anymore. He says my whipping up a perfect pot roast and scalloped potatoes makes the WASP wives squirm in their seats. Heaven forbid I ever make a rich white woman uncomfortable.

"This is delicious, dear," Camelia says. She is wearing a maroon pantsuit, a string of black pearls and far too much L'Air du Temps. "Very exotic." The sweetly compliant Young Asian Wife smiles and thanks her while emptying her own glass of Pinot Gris.

"Atomic bombs, now there's a whole other thing," booms Stuart. Beads of sweat line his broad forehead. "War. Escalation. Radiation. Some loony-tune in North Korea or somewhere in the Middle East pushes a button and it's all over. Kaboom! Done. So long, Charlie!" Stuart makes the motion of washing his hands of a situation.

"We visited the Middle East once," says Camelia. "Dreadful place!"

"It's unlikely an atomic war will do us in," I say. "It'll be something seemingly small, like the eventual extinction of honeybees. We'll all starve."

"More jasmine rice, Stuart?" David stiffly wipes his mouth with a napkin.

"Have you heard of colony collapse disorder?" I ask. "The bees die and there goes most of our food supply." I gesture to our table. "Cashews need to be pollinated. Green peppers, too."

"Honey, the bees will be fine," laughs David, embedding his elbow in the general area of Stuart's ribs, sheathed as they are in a dense, fleshy parabola. "They're nothing but pests, they'll stick around forever! Like cockroaches. There will be pesky bees buzzing about long after we're all dead. But go ahead and sign another online petition, babe."

"I saw a dead bee in the rose garden today," offers Camelia.

"I don't see why people are getting all frothed up about the extinction of some bloody insect or another." Stuart starts up again like a diesel lawn mower. "We can pollinate crops ourselves. With technology. Hell, even by hand! Saw it on the TV once. All of these hard-working Chinese on ladders – maybe even cousins of yours, eh, Min? – dipping feathers or paintbrushes or some such into apple blossoms. Pollinating them one at a time."

"Feathers." Camelia nods. "Paintbrushes." I pour myself another hefty glass of wine.

"Did you know," David tells them, "that we own five different can openers?"

"Five?" Camelia gasps. "What on earth for?"

"To be fair" – I feel my cheeks starting to get hot – "the electric one was a Christmas present from David's sister."

"And the other four?" Stuart's eyebrow seems to hover in mid-air.

"The other four don't need electricity." My voice is flat. I calmly gather up the empty dishes. "We'll need multiples down the road, because what if one breaks? What if two break? What if the pollinators all die and there aren't any fresh food sources left and all we have are cans but no can openers? We'd have to survive on whatever had been canned all the years before. Peaches and lentils and beets!"

"Oh my!" That was David. My husband could be clever sometimes. That's part of the reason why I fell for him in the beginning. His quick wit and unchecked confidence. I'm not a gold digger, but we were dirt poor growing up, so the fact that this witty, handsome silver fox happened to be a successful hedge fund manager was intoxicating. Instead of asking if he could buy me a drink when we first met, he asked if he could buy me the whole damned bar. But David has long since given up trying to impress me.

"My husband doesn't like for me to talk about my emergency preparedness," I say. I glide into the kitchen and place the dishes in the sink. I open a drawer and turn the faucet to full blast, hoping it's enough to mute the sound of the childproof cap popping off my bottle of Lorazepam. "He thinks it makes me seem crazy. But it's better to be prepared than to be caught off guard. Better to look silly than starve."

"You should see the storage room under our stairs," I hear David whisper to them conspiratorially. "Cases of bottled water everywhere."

"What do you think of this global warming I keep hearing about?" Camelia says as I take my seat next to her. "Melting icebergs and Swedish children being taken out of school and such." She gently shakes her bourbon glass so the cubes clack against themselves. An Orff ensemble in miniature. I look at her pinched, narrow face and absently wonder if she'd ever been beautiful. She's still thin, at least.

"You're worried about global warming after the wretched winters we've been having?" Stuart shakes his head. "Global warming is a scam perpetuated by leftists and social justice warriors! It's fake news."

"Fake news," echoes David.

"Utter hogwash!" says Stuart.

David pours more wine. "Dessert, anyone? Min makes a divine khanom krok."

"London will look so beautiful under water, don't you think?" I say dreamily. "Imagine Big Ben as the centrepiece of a new Atlantis."

"Har!" is Stuart's one-note response.

I look at him. "How long can you tread water, Stuart?"

"Honey, stop being so morbid."

"I'm being *realistic*," I tell David. "Everything ends."

"You're being morbid and dramatic and you actually sound like an insane person. Can we please change the subject." It is more command than question. Stuart and David go on to talk shop – dividends and pipelines and the gold standard. Camelia and I regard one another benignly. My wine-drunk mind flits about hazily, like a honeybee, from one cataclysmic thought to the next. I think about whales and dead fish washing up on shorelines, their stomachs full of plastic bags and tampon applicators. Dead birds dropping from the sky like hailstones. Mussels and oysters cooked in their shells without ever leaving the ocean. These are ominous harbingers of a slow systemic death much bigger than ourselves. Still, there's something sexy about it. Like how a highway car crash or forest fire can be bizarrely exciting.

Camelia is showing me photos of their recent Kenyan safari on her phone. Now she is showing me photos of their nine grandchildren. Nine grandchildren seem like altogether too large a progeny – especially when it comes to Stuart and Camelia's lacklustre genes and low intelligence.

"Julia, our youngest, is pregnant with our tenth!" she announces proudly, waving her phone in my face. Pregnant Julia is blonde and generic-looking. She's the kind of person you'd have to meet several times before remembering her name.

The men talk over us. Stuart is getting louder and louder. David enthusiastically agrees with everything he says.

There's something in my chest, a feather in my rib cage. It tickles and I giggle. It's square on my chest now and I have to get it off. I have to get it off of me because I've kept it in for so long now and I will otherwise jump out of my skin. "Did you know –" I laugh "– that David can't get me pregnant?"

Suddenly, I have everyone's full attention.

"Oh, he's tried and tried, you know! Poor dear! I know it's not me, because . . . well, let's just say that I know. Good at stocks, bad at storks, aren't you, darling? And did you know he's too stubborn and too proud to even go to the doctor about it?"

"Min." David's eyes are saucer wide.

"Maybe we should try feathers, darling! Oh, I know! Let's try paintbrushes!" I laugh harder, looking from David to Stuart, Stuart to Camelia, Camelia to David. Dinner is over.

The apocalypse won't happen all at once. It will unfold slowly, over time. Flood waters rising molasses-slow and wildfires digesting the rest until there is nowhere left to migrate. We'll tell ourselves that everything is fine until there is no air left to breathe, no swollen body of water left unpoisoned. Civilization will come apart more slowly than a marriage rotting from the inside out; our usual way of life dwindling until there's nothing left. Just nothing left at all.

Everyone You Love Is Dead

RENBOURN, DOROTHY. *Peacefully in her sleep in her 76th year. Devoted wife to Douglas Renbourn, JD. Beloved "mumsy" to furbaby Denton von Woofington III. Dorothy loved animals and was a devoted volunteer at the Toronto Humane Society. Friends are invited to the visitation tomorrow 6PM–8PM at Magdalene Funeral Home on Steeles Avenue. Interment will take place at St. Paul's Cemetery on Wednesday morning at 11 o'clock. Coffee and light refreshments will be served. In lieu of flowers, donations to the Toronto Humane Society would be gratefully appreciated by the family.*

DOROTHY LOOKS GOOD. NATURAL. HECK — ALMOST youthful! You never know what you're going to get with these funeral home makeup artists nowadays. The homes have all been outsourcing the cosmetic work to freelancers because full-time staffers cut into the bottom line. Instead of hiring staff to sit around all hours of the day watching their nails dry, now the homes pay contractors per cadaver. It makes sense from a business perspective, but you *would not believe* the hatchet jobs I've seen! Most of them just look bad. There was this one corpse – Olive something, schoolteacher – anyway, Olive was a *goddamned mess*. The woman was eighty-seven years old and was tarted up like a Louisiana hooker during Mardi Gras. Gobs of eyeshadow. Red lipstick. Rouge to *here*. Eyelashes like spiders! She was in a state, that poor Olive, I tell you! I felt so sorry for her poor husband. I couldn't close with him. He was too distraught. I assume her horrifically clown-like appearance had something to do with it.

Now Dorothy here – she's a work of art! Looks like she's just sleeping, honestly. Ol' Dorothy supposedly kicked it in her sleep, too, which is exactly the way you want to go. People of the world: get yourselves a nocturnal heart attack – gone before you even know what's what.

I imagine Douglas woke up without an alarm at six in the morning as he always does, saw his wife lying there beside him, kissed her gently on the forehead and decided to let her sleep in. He'd shake out a piss, head down to the kitchen (renovated just last year after decades of indecision and discussion), put on a pot of coffee and maybe wait for her to descend the creaky wooden staircase of their century home to fix the soft-boiled eggs and oatmeal they'd been enjoying together every morning for their decades of married life.

But ol' Dorothy never came downstairs. He'd discover she went to the Big Upstairs instead.

Or maybe Douglas never ate breakfast in the mornings. Maybe it was Denton von Woofington III who discovered her body. Douglas was already arriving at work in his freshly pressed shirt and tie, battered leather briefcase in tow – his colleagues at the firm wondering with some bitterness when the man was finally going to retire – and Denton's relentless barking and whining eventually brought the next-door neighbours knocking. Unable to get a hold of Douglas, they'd used the spare key under the welcome mat (there's always a spare key under the welcome mat) to find the cocker spaniel (it's always a cocker spaniel) whining and licking his mumsy's slack, grey face.

There's another strong possibility, however. It's that Dorothy didn't die in her sleep at all. What a calm and lovely narrative that is – peacefully shuffling off this mortal coil in the middle of the night. "I woke up and she was already gone." Zero feathers ruffled. It's possible – and don't think this doesn't happen with great frequency – that ol' Dorothy and Douglas were getting frisky in the early a.m. hours, if you know what I mean. (That little blue pill changed everything!) Suddenly, the woman currently laid out in the mahogany box clutched at her crepey chest, crying out for reasons unrelated to sexual climax (rare) or the faking of sexual climax (more frequent) and ol' Dorothy breathes her last, God rest her eternal soul. Douglas – raised staunchly Catholic, for the record – quickly dresses his late wife in the most puritanical nightgown in her wardrobe (white flannel! sleeves!) while waiting for the ambulance to arrive. He would think to do this before it even occurs to him that he should search the dusty filing drawers of memory to remember how to do C P R. But the thought of strangers gaping at his wife's naked body was simply too much for his Catholic shame to bear. And how could he ever explain the crotchless panties to the paramedics?

Dorothy is wearing a smart forest-green suit, a string of cultured pearls, earrings to match and her wedding ring. I always steal a glance at the hands of the deceased. If the wedding ring is present, the widower is the sentimental type and it's unlikely he'll be interested in what I have on offer. If the wedding ring is absent, the widower is a more practical sort of man and it's almost guaranteed he'll be game. My success rate for ring-is-gone types is nearly perfect.

Douglas cuts an impressive figure in his slate-grey suit and royal blue tie. Not the usual boring black-suited fustiness. He's a good-looking guy for his age. Tall. That's always good.

I go to the ladies' room to powder my nose and give myself a quick once-over before the Approach. I'm not as young as I used to be, but I still look like the kind of woman men would cheat on their wives with, with barely a second thought. Big tits, small waist. That's more than enough, isn't it?

I smack my lips together in the mirror. Russian Red. Wearing it makes me feel like a wartime spy.

"Mr. Renbourn" – I attach a cool, manicured hand to his wrist – "I am sincerely sorry for your loss. Your wife was very dear to me. Very dear."

"Thank you," says Douglas. "I'm sure you were very dear to her, as well."

"I'd like to think so," I say. "We volunteered together at the humane society."

"Oh, of course," says Douglas. His face is flushed. Good sign. "Dodobird was always telling me about all of the lovely people she met over there."

"It won't be the same without her."

The next part of our conversation is always the same. It's the same at every visitation, every funeral, every memorial service I've ever attended in this capacity. It could be scripted. Just a word or two off, but it's essentially the same interaction, time and time again. It's remarkable.

"I'm sure she would have been touched by your presence here, Mrs. . . . ?"

"Oh, I'm not married," I'll say.

"Attractive young lady like you?" they'll say. "Why on earth not?"

"I was engaged, once," I'll say. "Everyone I love is dead."

"Me too," they'll say with downcast eyes. Then they'll look back into mine, searching. And I'll know I have them.

That's it. Right there. The point of connection. We're just a couple of lonely sad sacks free-falling our way through a cruel and unfeeling universe. I haven't got a husband. They haven't got a wife. Not anymore. Whether or not we have children or friends or Denton von Woofington III, we're all alone in this life and we both know it.

Yes. We truly understand each other.

That's when I go in for the kill.

"I'm Rosemarie but you can call me Rosie," I say. "All my friends do."

"I'm happy to hear we're friends, Rosie. I'm Douglas."

"Pleasure, Douglas." I lean in close, conspiratorially. "Dorothy never told me she was married to such a handsome man."

Don't look at me like that. I know! You don't have to tell me because I already know. It's not right! It's not kind! They're so vulnerable at this moment! But I tell you, I promise you, I'm doing them a favour here. This is a win-win situation. I'm looking out for my own interests and they're in withdrawal of female companionship. Female care. Female nurturing.

Lucky for them: I happen to be female.

Please believe me when I tell you that most of these sad old guys don't know how to do their own laundry. Hell, they barely know how to boil spaghetti! These grown men are flailing, drowning, helpless children without their wives to grease the gears of their everyday lives. If they don't have an adult daughter willing to sacrifice her remaining fertile years to help take care of daddy at home, they're screwed. And they know it.

Enter a beautiful and busty stranger at their wife's funeral. She takes the widower aside and gives them a bit of attention and compassion. She offers up compliments like Pez candies, one by one by one. This beautiful (and busty) stranger opens the door to a mild flirtation and perhaps ends the most terribly stressful day of this man's life with some kissing and maybe a friendly little tug in the private powder room – more a therapeutic massage, really. Who can blame these men? Who can blame them for wanting to be on the receiving end of such attention and affection and care? And who can blame me for wanting to provide it? I'm practically performing a public service!

Due to their generally advanced age and the mountain of stress they've been dealing with, the massages don't always take but the recipient is always extremely appreciative. Some of them weep afterwards, from gratitude, grief or relief. They take my business card in a daze, which is just my name and phone number, white and mauve. I ask them to call me and they always do. Sometimes they call the very next day. Wifey dead and buried. Time to bury something else?

Not so fast.

The widower will always suggest treating me to dinner. (This older generation, I tell you! They should teach classes to the young.) I'll downgrade this offer to a coffee, much to his disappointment. I'll shake his hand formally upon greeting him, as though we were meeting for the first time. As though we hadn't had our little tousle. I'll tell him I'm single at the moment, but I'm not looking to get involved with a man who isn't ready to date, his loving wife's body barely cold. I'm open to new friends, however, and I felt our connection was undeniable.

So, whaddaya say? Friends?

Friends, you should hear what happens next. It would turn your blood cold. I get all sorts of protests. Sometimes angry, sometimes weepy. He insists he is ready to date. *He is ready to date!* His marriage was a sham, practically. It was a marriage in name only. He couldn't remember the last time his wife had touched him the way I'd touched him at her wake, but it was probably when Reagan was in office. They were friends, mostly. Just companions, honestly. Nodding acquaintances in the same household, if he's being completely honest. They stayed together for the house. They stayed together for the kids. They stayed together for their family, their friends, their neighbours, for money, for appearances. They stayed together out of *sheer goddamned inertia*.

No, there was nothing holding back his heart. He'll grip my hand as though it were the only thing keeping him from falling into the void of loneliness. He was ready. He had never been readier. He was finally free.

I smile gently and tell him I'm happy for him. I'm happy he's ready, I'm happy he's free. But I'm not sure we would work out.

He'll stare at me blankly. (Men aren't used to being on the wrong side of this speech.)

I explain again. Gently, firmly. Our chemistry is undeniable. Overwhelming, actually. But I'm not in a good place to date right now. Or possibly ever.

Confusion. Disappointment. A glimmer of entitled rage. A child on the cusp of shrieking for a toy he can't have. I can see it in their eyes. Their want.

"Listen, Douglas," I say. "I bet it would do you some good to get out there. I'd love for you to meet this single friend of mine."

His eyes light up in a vulpine way.

"Your friend, eh?" he'll say. "Tell me more."

No matter how smart they claim to be, when you really get down to it, most men are as predictable as rom-coms.

"She's beautiful. Successful. Owns her own home so she's not looking for a free ride. Just a nice time with a decent fella. And goodness gracious, she would just *love* you!"

"She would, eh?"

"Who wouldn't, darling?" I wink. "Just don't tell her how we met, okay?"

If there were a dotted line, he'd be slavering to sign it.

"Let me take care of all of the little details," I coo. "I owe you that much. I'll make the restaurant reservation and I'll even treat you two to a meal, as a *mea culpa* for my . . . lack of self-control. I want you to enjoy yourself! God knows you deserve a fun night out."

I look into his eyes and can almost see visions of sugar plum fairies and large-breasted women half his age dance in his head. Here's what he's thinking to himself. He's thinking, "If Rosie is in her thirties, how old could her friends possibly be?"

As soon as I get home and kick off my heels, I'm on the phone.

"Mavis, darling," I say. "It's Rosie. Have I got a live one for you!"

It's always such a novelty to find a single man in their age range who is actually – well – alive. After sixty-five or so, they all start dropping dead. And it's the single ones who die first.

43

"You'll be meeting him at Cabana Baby at 8:00 p.m. on Tuesday night. I'll make the reservation in your name. Dinner's on me. But do me a favour? This one's a friend of a friend and not a client, so don't tell him how we met, okay? He probably wouldn't agree to it, otherwise."

Where did I meet Mavis? It wasn't at her husband's funeral, that's for sure. It was at a tony lunch spot in Yorkville. Mavis wore frosted lipstick, had perfectly coiffed white hair and smelled like rosewater and money. Honest to god, she smelled like actual paper money. (When you grow up with nothing, the smell of money is the best smell in the world. I can suss it out like a starving bloodhound.) In shaky senior's scrawl, Mavis writes a cheque for fifty thousand dollars, made out to me. She draws a heart in the memo line. This cheque comes with the promise that I find her a boyfriend, a husband or at least a few nice men to go out with and show her a good time.

Your friend Rosie is a professional matchmaker. And it's my job to find successful older men for the rich older women – it's always women, only women – to date in order to fulfill our very expensive contract.

But the older women get, the fewer men there are. The older women get, the less desirable society deems them. They're not even desirable to men their own age. No matter how bald or lined or fat they themselves have become, men my clients' own age always seem to be chasing after women even younger than me. Sometimes, if they have money, they get them. And after age fifty-five or so, with very few exceptions, women become invisible. The men start dropping dead but it's the women who actually disappear.

How can I run a successful matchmaking business with that social structure in place? How do I keep two dozen loaded Eleanor Rigbys happy and occupied and twirling and whirling on a dance floor somewhere when the older men are either dead or disinterested? How can I live up to my campaign promises? This is why I pore over the obituaries every weekend. I seek out the widower doctors and lawyers, primarily. Quality men. Impressive men. Men who are worth every penny I charge.

"How did you hear about me, Mavis?"

"My realtor Deborah told me all about you," says Mavis. "Says you found her a man. But then I had my best friend's granddaughter look you up online to make sure you're legit."

"I'm legit as they come, Mavis. You're in good hands."

Douglas and Mavis will meet for dinner. Mavis will get a little tipsy and feel a bit sheepish afterwards. Douglas will be unfailingly polite. A gentleman. She's only a handful of years older than him, but she must seem like a crone. Especially after his big-titted sugar plum fantasies. Mavis must seem even worse than a crone. Mavis must seem like a sad joke. And he's the walking, talking punchline. He'll know I played him for a sucker. He'll feel neutered and humiliated. I try not to think about that part. I try not to think about the men's feelings. It's not the men I'm working for. It's the women I'm trying to help.

After her third squashed strawberry margarita, Mavis will ask Douglas to dance with her, dance with her, dance with her, please. He'll chuckle and make polite excuses. Bad back. Fallen arches. Bunions. He'll tell her he has to work early the next day. Mavis will understand. Her late husband had been exactly like that himself. These workaholics! She was used to them. Robbing herself of happiness for his sake, bending like a reed to accommodate his rigidity, that was their life together. She'd wanted children but he didn't. So they didn't have a child. She'd wanted a little cat, but he hadn't allowed for that either. All of that hair all over their draperies and upholstery! But they lived in a big, beautiful, immaculate house (a nice Filipino girl came twice a week to clean) and theirs was a happy enough life. Not that Mavis knew any different. Like some clever lizard, she had disappeared into the background of her husband's favourite beige wallpaper. And now that he was gone, she was searching for another man to please. Another man to be changed and smothered by. Another man who will want her to submit and bend like a reed.

I've never married. Will never marry. When people ask, I just tell them I haven't met the right man yet. But this is why. This is precisely why.

Mavis will call me excitedly the next day and let me know that Douglas was a dream. An absolute dream come to life, Rosie! Mavis sounds so good on the phone. Natural. Almost youthful. I'll encourage her. Bolster her confidence. Tell her exactly what she wants to hear. Because what she's paying for is hope. When everyone you love is dead and life's best stuff is behind you, hope is all you've got left. I can't sell her hope at this age, not really, but I can do my best to manufacture it.

I'm doing her a kindness, really. I tell myself this over and over again. It took me a bit of time to convince myself – years, if I'm being honest – but now I really and truly believe it. I'm doing all of them the very greatest kindness.

Like everything else, love is essentially a transaction. At the core of it, men want youth, beauty and access to sex.

And women? Women just want to be seen.

Even if they're only part of the scenery.

White Cake

I DID IT! I WON! FOR ONCE IN MY LIFE, I ACTUALLY won something!

So let me tell you how it all went. Donna and Judy organized a bake sale for the whole office. Before any goodies ever got sold, they were going to choose the best ones – the number one winners! My boss Mark plus Donna were the official judges (Judy has the diabetes) and they got to taste all the treats, those lucky ducks! It was all for fun and also so we could raise money for an important children's charity, can't remember which.

Anyway, the whole thing of it was that you had to make your goodies from scratch. Nothing out of a box. Nothing store-bought. *No Betty! No Duncan! No Cheating!* Isn't that just the cleverest? I wish I came up with it myself, but that's just what it said on the bake sale posters. (The posters were awfully cute, by the by; they had these little sparkly pink cupcakes with smiley faces on them. Just the happiest little cupcakes! Like they were positively *thrilled* they were going to get themselves eaten!) I should have saved one of the posters as a souvenir. I'll ask Judy tomorrow if she has any spare ones kicking around.

So they announce this bake sale and I get silly excited! I can't even stop thinking about it! I search through my recipe books at home trying to find something that would wow them, like really knock their socks off, you know? I'm a good little baker, Darryl will tell you that much! But I wanted something real special this time. Something bonkers good and different. I asked Darryl what he thought, but he just kept watching TV and told me to just shut up about the stupid baking contest already. Grumpus von Lumpus! Anyway, I'm practically climbing the walls at home, so I drive to the No Frills across the way, buy armfuls of whatever I feel like and when I get home, I just whip it all up together to see what the heck would come of it. Just like on those food survivor shows! (Can I be really bad for a second? My favourite episodes are the ones with the cute little kids who cry and cry when they get sent home. I know! So bad! Bad Carol!)

If I'm being honest – and I always am – it really felt like I was baking something special this time. Something magical. I felt a bit like an artist or a famous painter! Like the Group of Seven, except there's only one of me! It's like my hands were on a Ouija board and they moved all on their own. To tell you the truth, I barely thought about what I was even doing at all! I popped a few different things in the oven, just really experimenting, you know? But the best-looking thing was this chocolate peanut butter pie that smelled just completely out of this world! I really should have written down the recipe as I was making it, but I bet you dollars to doughnuts, I could probably make it exactly the same way next time. I just have to get into "the zone," as Mark loves to say.

So the bake sale was supposed to start at twelve noon, but the judging happened fifteen minutes before and we could watch the whole thing happening, if we really wanted. I was so nervous all morning waiting for it to start. I sweat so much in my sparkly pineapple shirt (a gift from my sister Shelley from her trip to Maui) and had to go to the ladies' twice so I could stick my soggy armpits under the hand dryer.

I watched Mark like a hawk when he tasted my pie. He was supposed to keep a straight little poker face on him the entire time, but he let out this little puff of breath after taking a bite of my pie and his eyes rolled all the way up to the ceiling and I could tell! I could just tell! I knew right then that I was going to be the winner! But he didn't say boo. I just clapped my hands a little bit and stifled giggles.

And sure enough, I was right! There was a very special email at the end of the day that announced the winner. Donna won Most Beautiful Dessert (which I didn't think was very fair since she organized the sale and should have been disqualified, but her meringues were very professional looking, like something out of a fancy Martha Homemaker magazine or something). And guess what? My chocolate peanut butter pie won Best Tasting Dessert and Best Overall Dessert!

Goodness! I screamed and screamed when I saw the news (I was shushed by Marilyn in finance, but she's a real stick in the mud). I was just so thrilled! I mean, I kind of wish they'd've announced it out loud at a meeting or something so everyone could have clapped for me and I could have done a goofy little curtsy or something and maybe get pinned with a blue ribbon, but that email was pretty special, too. They changed the background and lettering and everything so it looked real pretty. It was all done up in the same colours as the posters: pinks and mauves and blues. It looked so nice that I even printed it out. My pie sold out in minutes, Mark told me! Twelve slices at three bucks a pop. That's me, myself and I raising a cool thirty-six dollars for all of those sweet little Mexican amputee orphans or whatever.

*

The next day, Mark called an emergency staff meeting for 10:00 a.m. in the boardroom. Not good, not good. Things hadn't been going so hot at work since even before that Japanese company bought us out. There had been some pretty drastic layoffs in the warehouse, I knew. I've been working here for almost seventeen years though, so I figured I must be safe enough. Was feeling sick and worried about the young people, though. First, to lose a baking contest (to me, the overall winner of the baking contest) and then to lose their jobs? The next generation really don't get a fair shake. Not at all. But at least they have their avocado toasts.

When the big hand pointed to twelve and the little hand pointed to ten, everyone headed to the boardroom and just kind of stood around, not knowing what to do or what to expect. We were all very quiet and nervous and looking around at each other. Mark comes in, looking all stiff and serious, which is odd because he's such a natural joker. And then Mark, he takes this deep breath and says that there's something very important that we need to discuss as a group, and I could feel everyone's hearts beating just a little bit louder. My armpits were feeling so sweaty again and I wished I could leave the meeting for a sec to give them a good blast under the hand dryer. That's when Mark busted out into this huge smile and he said, "Congratulations to Carol Orfus for winning yesterday's bake sale and to all of us for raising two hundred dollars for super sad-eyed orphans in Madagascar or whatever!" (Not what he said, just how my brain remembers it!) What an absolute ham! It was a good emergency meeting after all! So everyone laughs and there's a bit of applause for me and I start whooping and giggling like crazy! And then! Mark, he presents me with all of these prizes! A Pharmastone coffee mug (now I have two!) and a Pharmastone key chain, which is just the cutest thing, you should see it! It's made up to look like a little prescription pill bottle, but instead of being full of pills, it's full of these little pink and blue candies. Really clever! And then Mark's new assistant, this really pretty young Oriental woman, pins me with a blue ribbon that says WINNER on it.

"Congratulations, Carol," she says. I would say thank you and her name, only I don't know her name because she only started a couple of weeks ago. So I just giggle some more. Anyway, Mark gets all worked up and starts chanting, "Speech! Speech! Speech!" And I am blushing *just so hard,* so all I can say is thanks. Thanks! Thank you so much, everyone! And then I curtsy and everyone claps again and cheers for me and I yell out, "I'm a master baker!" and everyone laughs and I laugh, too.

It felt just wonderful. I wish Darryl could've seen all the fuss they made over me, it was really *quite* something!

Afterwards, Jamie (that's the name of the pretty little Oriental gal, I later found out) comes by my desk and asks if I'd like to have lunch with her that afternoon. And I know this sounds silly, but I felt kind of special to be asked by such a lovely young lady if I'd like to have lunch with her. And so I say yes and when noon rolls around, I drive us both to Mr. Burger (it's the only place around here that isn't ethnic food, which I'm not overly keen on) and Jamie and I have such a lovely time! She asks me all kinds of questions about my baking and also about Pharmastone, since I've been working here for so long. She also asks a lot of questions about Mark, because she wants to be the very best assistant she can be. What a little go-getter! I tell Jamie that Mark is a complete and total sweetheart and such a silly goose! And because she asks, I also tell her about how he's married to a woman named Deborah and they have two little girls and they live by the water in Mimico in a huge, lovely home. Plus, they have a pool. (I haven't actually been invited over to see the house, but I hear it's really something else!)

Anyway, Jamie and me, we're chatting and joking and giggling just like old school pals! I think I might have made a real office friend! Not that I'm not friends with just about everybody in the office, I mean, they're all just so nice (with the exception of Marilyn in finance), but I mean like a real close office buddy and confidante.

*

I was in such a good mood that evening that I made some molasses cookies to take into work the next day. Darryl wasn't thrilled that I made cookies for my office instead of a proper dinner for him, but never mind to him! I opened a can of tomato soup and made him some toast.

"You're not going to starve to death," I tell him, gently patting him on his spare tire.

"You're one to talk," he says.

*

Everybody at work loved my cookies. And I mean *loved*!

"You're turning into quite the Betty Crocker, aren't you, Carol?" says Mark. I couldn't have been happier if he had given me a raise. (Well, maybe a little bit happier. But not by much.)

My beautiful new office friend Jamie absolutely loved the cookies, too. She gushed and gushed about them and asked me for the recipe at our next lunch date. She also asked a little bit more about Mark's wife – what she does for a living, what she looks like. I couldn't really say, to be honest. I have always pictured her as a blonde. Mark doesn't keep any photos of his family in his office, is the thing. He likes to tell people he just hates clutter! Heck, the guy doesn't even have a plant! (I have three. All cacti.)

"I'm a minimalist, Carol," Mark told me when I asked about that. "I'm such a minimalist that I think Philip Glass is a little too much!" And then he laughed and I laughed too, even though I didn't really understand the joke. I honestly thought Philip Glass was a windshield company. I felt so stupid when I got back to my desk and did a Bing search.

Well now, and here's some office gossip! Jamie's engaged! She keeps the ring on a necklace around her neck (which is why a busybody like me never noticed it before) and she showed me photos of her fella on her fancy phone. He is an Oriental gentleman. Handsome, like Bruce Lee. I told her that they were going to make the cutest little babies! Chinese babies really are just the cutest things in the world, next to little Black babies with their sweet fluffy lamb hair and also cat babies (kittens). White babies all just kind of look like drunk old politicians to me, with their double chins, baldness and red, angry faces. Not cute! Nope! None for me, thanks!

When I got home, I told Darryl about my new work friend and how she's just the most gorgeous little girl you ever did lay your eyes on.

"Orientals are a damned ugly breed," he says.

I tried to explain to him that he's *very* wrong.

"Jamie has perfect skin and lovely almond-shaped eyes and cascades of the shiniest hair imaginable. It's like she's a porcelain doll come to life! Just perfect. Perfect.

"And *besides*," I say to Darryl, "aren't you forgetting a certain someone named Lucy Liu?"

I couldn't stay cranky, though. I got a postcard from Shelley in Bermuda! That sister of mine is always travelling to such nice places. She's done very well for herself, that one. And without a husband, even! How do you like that? I'm not going to paste the postcard in my scrapbook, though, because if I glued it down one way, I'd ruin her writing and if I glued it down the other way, I'd ruin the lovely photo of a seashell and sunglasses on perfect white sand. (Life's a Beach, it says. I read it out to Darryl. "Life's a beach and then you die," he grumbled and I smacked him so hard on the arm that he spilled a bit of his beer on the arm of the couch.) So anyway, Shelley's postcard will sit on our coffee table for now. Maybe it'll remind Darryl that we haven't been on a proper vacation in a long time. Hint, hint, Mr. Husband!

Shelley is a spinster, but I would never call her that to her face. That is hurtful. Like me and Darryl, she is also childless.

"Childless?" My sister threw back her head and laughed. "More like child-free, Carol!"

Child-free! I liked that. Kind of like caffeine-free. Or sugar-free, ha! Child-free makes it seem like Darryl and I have saved ourselves from the hard work of becoming parents and take trips to Italy twice a year instead. (We've never been to Italy, I should say. But we have dined at an Olive Garden just outside of Fort Lauderdale, and the food and climates are really quite similar.) Maybe I'll ask Darryl about taking a trip to Italy this year to celebrate "child-free."

*

Jamie introduced me to sushi. Can you believe it? Me eating raw fish! I don't even like cooked fish! But you know what, it wasn't half bad! I let Jamie order for me and she swore up and down that I wouldn't get sick from mercury poisoning afterwards. I tried the California rolls, which were okay and not too fishy. I also tried these deep-fried vegetables called tempura. I explained to Darryl that they were kind of like Japanese French fries. Just delicious! Jamie ordered more exotic choices for herself, ahem. She asked me if I wanted to try some eel and I just about keeled over. Me? Eat eel? No thank you very much! I'd rather an eel eat me than the other way around!

Jamie and I got to talking about her life a little more on this outing. "Speaking of Japanese food and the Japanese," I say to her. "Is that how you got hired here, Jamie? Family, maybe?"

"Pardon?" Jamie blinks. I tell her, in case she didn't know, that a big Japanese company recently bought Pharmastone.

"My parents immigrated from South Korea," Jamie says.

"Oh, sorry!" I say. "I knew you were an Oriental, at any rate."

Jamie then tells me that she applied for her job on Workopolis and that *Oriental* isn't a word that people use anymore. People are supposed to say *Asian* now. And she tells me that she is Canadian, born in Canada. I thank her for the information. I can never keep up with all of the new politically correct slang! Some days, I feel like such a retard!

Jamie seemed pretty stressed out during our lunch. She's usually so sweet and smiley but she seemed kind of tired and quiet and distant as we headed back to the office. I started to wonder if Mark's been working the poor thing too hard. I decided I'd have to keep a closer eye on that.

*

My second-try soufflé turned out perfect! Just perfect! I was the belle of Pharmastone HQ, if I do say so! Mark even emailed me all special-like to "commend" (his word) the master baker on her "masterpiece." What a guy! Funny and smart!

My friends at the office nearly made up for Darryl being an old crankypants lately. But maybe I deserve it. I have been getting so wrapped up in baking treats lately that it would completely slip my mind to make him dinner. That day, I was still full from my Asian feast with my new Canadian-Korean friend. So I threw some hamburger into a frying pan at ten at night after he complained, and he didn't even bother touching it! Just tossed it straight into the trash! Said he wasn't hungry anymore. I cried a little at the waste of it all. Darryl hasn't worked for a few years now and money can be tight sometimes. I swear, that hubby of mine can be such a handful! It might be good that we're child-free because I'm certainly not Darryl-free. One spoiled, whiny baby at home is more than enough for this old gal.

When I told Jamie about how Darryl has been hell on wheels lately, she was such a good and kind listener. She kept saying to me, "Oh Carol, I know! Men!" and "It's really not your fault at all," and it was all just so soothing. It's so good to talk about woman things with another woman who understands. And she's so good at changing the subject when I get too sad or worked up, usually back to our friend Mark, who I also looooooooove to talk about. We're such terrible gossips, we Pharmastone girls!

Speaking of gossip, Jamie told me something at lunch that I knew I needed to keep to myself. I shouldn't even tell Darryl. So it'll be our little secret.

Okay. Are you ready for this?

So I tell Jamie that she has the most beautiful and perfect eyebrows that I have ever seen and she just about floors me with her response.

"They're tattooed on," she says.

Tattoos, can you *believe* it! What a bad girl, I thought! But it gets even kookier still!

"I actually have alopecia," she says.

"Oh, I hear that it's very common," I tell her. "Come on over for dinner sometime and I'll fry you up a nice beef liver!"

Jamie laughs as if I told the funniest joke in the world. "No, Carol. Not anemia. Alopecia. It means I've lost all of my hair."

So then Jamie reaches up like she's going to scratch her head and pulls her hair off, and I mean all of it! Her beautiful shiny hair is just a wig and underneath it, she is as bald as an old man. I have to tell you the truth, I was a little bit shocked! I looked all around the restaurant to see if people were staring at Jamie's bald noggin, but nobody else seemed to notice or care at all.

I asked her all sorts of questions about it and she answered with the patience of a saint. No, it didn't hurt at all when her hair fell out. Yes, it might grow back, but probably not. Once I was more comfortable, she let me touch her head. It was smooth like a baby's bum. When we finished lunch, Jamie put the wig back on and let me adjust it for her so she didn't have to head to the ladies' room to make it look just right.

Then, Jamie asked something that made me so happy. Her future mother-in-law is throwing her a bridal shower on Saturday and she was wondering if I might bake the cake for the party. My goodness! I just about shrieked my head off, I was so thrilled! Jamie shushed me, but she was laughing too. She said that she couldn't pay me much for it, but I interrupted to tell her that the cake would just be a bridal shower present to her from her best-ever work buddy and she beamed. She wrote her mother-in-law's address down on a little Post-it Note and asked if I wouldn't mind delivering the cake between noon and one o'clock on Saturday. I asked Jamie what I should wear to the party and she explained that the shower is really just for family, but she'd bring some special top-secret leftovers to work on Monday so I could quietly celebrate with her all the same. A top-secret special celebration for just the two of us! I almost teared up with joy!

As we walked to the car, Jamie and me, I felt the craziest feeling in my chest, like a warm fluttery sort of melted-butter feeling. It was a thing I haven't felt in a long time. I think that feeling came from liking Jamie just so much, and a kind of special pride that she had chosen me to be her close personal bosom work friend. I felt so blessed. Just so darned lucky and blessed.

*

When I got home that night, I was in such a good mood that I baked up a batch of my special lemon meringue tarts and also whipped up my moist perfect marble cake as a little something extra for the crew at work.

"We're going to have to start calling you Julia Child around here, Carol Orfus!" Mark said. "You should have your own pastry shop! Better yet, your very own baking show!" And I laughed my head off. Imagine! Me on a television show! What a character, that Mark! He's the one who should be on TV with all of his perfect hair and face!

Jamie and me emailed all day long, figuring out the kind of cake that would be best for her bridal shower and it was no easy feat, I tell you what! Jamie's mother isn't a fan of chocolate (which I found pretty shocking – who doesn't love chocolate?) and her fiancé's sister is allergic to strawberries.

We figured it all out, though. We decided on a Meyer lemon cake with raspberry jam and a vanilla bean fondant icing. I said I should maybe write *Shower of Happiness* on the cake because that's what it says on all of the shower cakes I've seen at the Loblaws, but Jamie said she'd rather it be minimalist. No writing, none at all.

"Less is more," Jamie said, smiling.

Another postcard from Shelley arrived today. I wanted to remind Darryl that it's high time we planned a thrilling vacation of a lifetime for ourselves. I was going to talk to him about it right that second, but he was already asleep.

*

I was so excited to get home on Friday so I could bake Jamie's bridal shower cake. I was just rarin' to go so I rushed on out of the office! I was more than halfway home when I realized that I had left my good springform pan at work, the one I would need to make Jamie's cake, so I did a U-ey and headed on back.

The main doors of our building automatically lock at five thirty sharp every day, you see, but I went around the back and told Joyce in shipping about my pan. I've known Joyce for twelve years. She's a good egg, that one. Joyce used her security card to get in me through the back way.

I went upstairs and got my pan from the sink of the office kitchen. It still had bits of marble cake crusted on it, but I figured I'd just give it a good solid soak when I got home.

That's when I heard the voices. They were coming from the boardroom, which is attached to the kitchen by a door that's usually open.

What I heard was a woman's voice and a man's voice. I heard the woman's voice shrieking "Master baker! Master baker!" over and over. The man's voice was laughing all low and then the woman was laughing too.

I tippytoed over to the boardroom and rested my ear against the door. More laughter, and then muffled sounds like words and they sounded exactly like this:

Used to call her . . . Amorphous Orfus – man voice.
Oh (muffle), that's cruel! – lady voice.

Kind soul . . . not the sharpest knife . . . – man.
Master baker! and she didn't even . . . – lady.

Couldn't possibly be talking about me. No no no, of course not. Must be talking about someone else.

I watched as my hand twisted the doorknob. My brain really didn't want me to open that door but my body couldn't help itself. It was like one of those out-of-body-experience-type things again. Ouija board hands. Baking up treats, opening closed doors. Doing things Carol Orfus would never, never do.

So I opened the door. Slowly, quietly. And that's when I saw them on the boardroom table. Jamie was all kinds of bare naked. Her back to me, all pretty and pale, but it was my friend Jamie for sure. Her shiny dark wig hair shimmering and shimmying all down her shoulders. Mark stretched out on the boardroom table below her, his hairy legs pointing toward me.

I slammed the door shut and walked out of the building. I didn't even say bye to Joyce.

I don't remember the drive, but somehow I did get home. I got home and I baked a cake. I baked the best cake that I have ever baked in my life. Golden and gorgeous and raspberry jammy. I decorated it with the tiniest and most perfect pink rosettes I have ever made, and pretty polka dots that I made using the candies from my Pharmastone keychain after I smashed it open on the countertop with Darryl's hammer.

But again, the whole time I baked, I felt like my own body wasn't even mine. Like, I watched hands whipping the cake batter and hands putting my springform pan into my oven and hands smashing the keychain I had won in the bake-off and hands decorating the cake once it was cool, but it's like my hands belonged to somebody else. Some ghost or some person who was not me, who had nothing to do with me.

And then my stranger hands wrote this in lovely rosy icing:

Jamie

Fucked

Her Boss

At twelve o'clock, I drove up to my friend Jamie's mother-in-law's house and put the cake on the front stoop. I rang the doorbell twice. And then I drove away.

When I got home, Darryl was sprawled on the bathroom floor.

*

The nurse has given him something that keeps him quiet and comfy and still. He's asleep and his mouth is wide open but he's not snoring like usual, because there's a plastic mask over his face most of the time. He reminds me of a baby bird. All weak and helpless and depending on his mama bird to keep him from falling out of the nest and shattering his fragile bones on the ground.

I am going to let you in on a little secret: I don't love Darryl.
I don't think I've ever loved Darryl. Not even at the beginning.
But I married him anyway. Isn't that the silliest thing you've
ever heard? But now, things feel different. Seeing him all weak
and ill like this, wires and things hanging out of him, keeping
him alive after that heart attack? Today is the day I officially
love my Darryl. We've been married for thirty-four years and
this is the first time I have ever felt this way for him. I wish it
could be like this forever. I'd like to just freeze time. His lashes
are fluttering because he's dreaming, and I feel like my heart
might burst wide open. It's almost like my chest can't contain
it all. All of this feeling. Darryl is quiet and I am at peace. It's
just the most beautiful moment.

I watch as my Ouija hands, full of love and gentleness, reach
over to firmly cinch shut the tube on Darryl's oxygen mask. It
makes the same sound as my tangled-up vacuum hose. Darryl
coughs. Darryl wheezes. His eyes fly open and go wide. If he
weren't so darned medicated, he'd probably be shouting for a
nurse right now.

"It's okay," I tell him. "It's okay, Darryl. I love you."

After the funeral and all that jazz, I'll meet up with Shelley
on an island in Greece and bake her the most beautiful golden
honey cake. Or maybe I'll learn how to bake baklava – that's
the Greek version of pie, you know. We'll eat it while laughing
and listening to that funny bouzouki music and watching the
ocean glitter and glimmer under a beautiful pink and blue
layer cake sky.

I'll definitely write as many postcards as I possibly can, although I don't know who I'd send them to, to be honest. I think I'll probably just wind up sending them to myself. Nobody loves getting a nice postcard in the mail more than yours truly, if you can believe it.

Tiny Girls

MOTHER BELIEVED IN TCHOTCHKES MORE THAN she believed in her own diagnosis.

Bisque porcelain angels, blown glass ballerinas and salt and pepper shakers shaped like nesting hens constantly materialized on every available surface of our home. When the oncologist told her she had maybe six months to live, she picked up the pace. Every other day, a new package would arrive from eBay or the Home Shopping Network, emblazoned with a warning: FRAGILE.

"You can't take them with you, Mother."

"I'm not planning on going anywhere, Glenny," she said. As though the collective presence of a hundred ceramic clowns and litters of mismatched hodgepodge cats would be enough to weigh down her corporeality, keeping her anchored in the material world for good.

Mother's favourite knick-knacks were a pair of Harlequin clown bookends she'd picked up at an antiques mall in Temecula. The black-and-white monstrosities lounged in their place of honour on the mantle. Their use was form over function; instead of holding books in place, they pressed up against one another with nothing separating them. As something of an inside joke to myself, I once sandwiched a copy of *Either/Or* between them. I mostly wanted to see how long it would take her to notice. Mother promptly returned the tome to my room, complete with a Post-it Note asking that I store my books on my bookshelf, please, where they belong.

And then there were the porcelain dolls. She'd been collecting those for years. There were so many, they required their own bedroom. Rows upon rows of pretty little dolls in bonnets and bows, dolls with unblinking blue eyes, dolls wearing white lace dresses, extravagant plum velvet gowns or nothing at all.

Mother had named each of her tiny girls. Jacqueline and Suzanne. Sharon, Miranda and Janet. And sweet little Ruth, her favourite one of all.

"Glenny, angel," she said. "Grab me Meryl, would you please?"

She would then proceed to have a full one-sided conversation with the doll as though the object were a dear old acquaintance she'd run into at the supermarket.

"You're looking very well today, dear. Now, I hate to be the one to tell you this, but I'm afraid that handsome Victor Newman has amnesia again . . ."

Mother was a touch odd herself, so I suppose I've come by my own strangeness honestly.

I'm a professional student with a collection of my own. Unlike Mother's collection, mine was not kept in plain sight, but rather, on my computer's hard drive. Thousands of photos of little girls. Like Mother, I'd named them all.

Sandra and Danielle. Sweet Cindy. Little Jasmine. And perfect Rebecca, my favourite one of all. Girls in bonnets and bows, girls with unblinking blue eyes, girls wearing white lace dresses, extravagant plum velvet gowns or nothing at all.

Before I continue, let me state for the record that I am not a monster. I'm disgusted at myself and my proclivities. I've never acted on these urges, would never act on them. I am a 100 percent certified non-practising pedophile. I've loved my little darlings often, but only inside my head. I relieve my hideous desires with the aid of my imagination and pixels on a screen. That's it. That's as far as it has gone or ever will go.

If you knew me, you'd know the absolute last thing I am is stupid. I am entirely aware I am culpable on some level. I'm guilty simply by being a consumer of such images. But Humbert Humbert I am not. I am incapable of physically harming a child. I wouldn't hurt a fly. I'm vegetarian, for crying out loud! And a virgin. I've long since realized that the best way to not be led into temptation is to avoid it entirely. Entirely.

One of the most interesting things I learned in high school was that post-adolescent girls do not interest me in the least. The folds of flesh and fat and hair that make up sexually mature female bodies held little appeal for me. If I'm being brutally honest, I find adult women repulsive. There are no children in academia. Academia, therefore, was a safe place for me. Naturally, I remained there for as long as possible.

An undergraduate degree in English Literature was followed by a Master in Philosophy, which was followed by a Ph.D. in Eastern Philosophy. Twelve years of my life, an incalculable debt load and three impractical pieces of paper to show for it all.

I completed a series of internships after graduation, but nothing ever came of them. Just as well. I was badly needed at home when Mother got sick the first time and then, again, this second time. I kept her company, cooking and cleaning when she didn't have the energy to insist on doing it herself. Full-time caregiver is a respectable vocation – and it keeps me out of trouble.

We've gotten on each other's nerves, of course. I wished she'd stop smoking. She wished I'd leave the house, maybe go on a date or two. ("Here's $20," she'd write on a Post-it Note occasionally, stuck to a bill. "Take some lucky girl out for a slice of pizza.") I wished she'd talk less. She wished I'd talk more. But neither of us changed a thing. People never change, not really.

It was a Saturday. Mother said she was feeling better than she had in weeks. She made a few calls and decided to attend an estate sale with a friend of hers.

"Bargoons galore, Glenny!" she'd always say. "Their loss is my gain!"

I dropped Mother off just before 10:00 a.m. I was to pick her up at half past one, after she and Doris had had their lunch. I was looking forward to spending those hours on the computer in peace with my girls. My sad-eyed, beautiful, wretched companions.

I'd just booted up the computer in the basement when the doorbell rang. I would have ignored it had it not rung again in short succession another ten or fifteen times.

Expecting to see a pair of older women proffering religious tracts, I was already making my excuses and apologies when I was startled silent by the cherubic faces of two little blonde girls in green-and-white uniforms.

"Wanna buy some Girl Scout cookies, mister?" they asked in stereo, penetrating my soul with their blue laser beam gazes. Their name tags read *Joni* and *Janis*.

"Uh, no. No thank you. Not just now."

"Oh, come on, mister!" The one called Joni pouted. "It's for a good cause!"

The girls had been wearing matching knapsacks. Black and fuchsia, sagging at the top, almost as big as they were. I remember that detail, now. Assuming they were at least halfway through their cookie run, the vessels wouldn't have been stuffed to capacity with Girl Scout cookie boxes. There would have been room for some other things. Three dolls each, perhaps.

"I'm afraid I don't have any money. So you'd best just be on your ..."

The girls wormed themselves past me, making their way into the house.

"Holy moly, Joni! Look!"

When I whirled around, the Girl Scouts were already fondling Mother's glossy life-sized ceramic Irish setter.

"There's a good puppy. There's a good dog."

"Don't touch that!" I said. "Get out of here!"

They looked dismayed but backed off.

"Please, I'll be late for work. I need you to leave, please."

Their attentions were now focused on me.

"You wear your hair like a girl!" Joni shrieked, indicating the ponytail I've had since my undergraduate degree. "That's so funny!"

"Long hair isn't just for girls, you know."

"Yes, it is!"

"No, it's not."

"Fine." Then, under her breath, "Yes, it is."

Joni was clearly the ringleader. Janis was quieter. More of an observer, really. Undoubtedly more intelligent. I liked Janis best.

I could smell them, now. An intoxicating blend of fabric softener and sun lotion. Suddenly dizzy, I sat down. Where in God's name was their mother? I had to get these girls out of the house as quickly as possible. But my challenge was this: I never wanted them to leave.

"Here's twenty bucks," I said, waving the bill in the air like a white flag. "I'll take four boxes. Two peanut butter, two chocolate mint. Now will you please just go?"

"You have so much cool stuff." Fearless Joni crawled up into my lap to grab the twenty, effectively stopping time. "Where did you get all of it?"

"Here and there," I said, carefully nudging her off of my lap with an elbow. "Would you like to see the best part?"

"Yeah!"

Before I knew what was happening, I had led these gorgeous, flawless nymphets to our spare bedroom. What on earth was I doing?

"I've never seen Barbies like *these* before!" Janis fixed her blue high beams on me. "Mister, boost me?"

I raised her up by her armpits – the only part of her body aside from the top of her head that I deemed safe to touch. As she kicked up one smooth leg, I caught the briefest glimpse of blue floral underwear. The room waved and undulated as though I stood behind glass at an aquarium. I was going to pass out. I was going to be sick. I was going to die courtesy of cardiac arrest.

"I wish you were mine," Janis whispered into the plastic conch of Suzanne's ear.

"How about I go brew some tea for a little tea party?" I offered nonchalantly. "We already have cookies!" I was sweating profusely by then. The girls were too entranced by their new porcelain playmates to answer definitively, so I slid out of the hot powdery bedroom of my very fantasies and into the artificially cool air of the hallway.

"No fair he gets to play with these cool dolls all the time," I could hear one of the girls saying as I gently shut the door. "He's a grown-up. Dolls aren't for grown-ups. They're for kids!"

Tumescent and anguished, I staggered over to the washroom. I had to make quick work of my raging erection and/or commit immediate seppuku with the sharpened end of a toothbrush – damned safety razors! I considered the logistics of taking my own wretched life without the poor girls discovering my pathetic remains – crawling into the deep freeze with a plastic bag over my head, perhaps? Locking the washroom door, running a nice warm bath and chasing every available pill in the medicine cabinet with mouthwash? It was a shame that we lived in a bungalow and not on the top floor of a nice, tall apartment complex. It was then that the telephone rang. It was Doris. Mother had collapsed at the estate sale and could I be an absolute dear and scurry over to the hospital right away, please? I bolted out of the house and jumped into my car. I don't know how long the Girl Scouts stayed alone in the room full of dolls, but when I returned, I could still pick up the hot scent of them on the stale air.

*

One week later, the police questioned me for nearly an hour about the dolls that had materialized on neighbourhood porches. Left behind like religious tracts were a brunette porcelain doll, a redhead, a bald newborn baby doll in her baptismal gown and a pair of blue-eyed blondes. It was eerie, neighbours remarked, how the dolls matched the physical appearances of the sweet little girls softly sleeping inside, safely tucked into their cribs and princess canopy beds.

"Parents in the community are very concerned, sir," said the wall-eyed Hispanic cop.

"Understandably, officer."

"So you don't deny the dolls belonged to you?" That was the female officer with the crewcut. She eyed me with suspicion. I had had nothing to do with this, but the sour shame around what I *could* have done to those innocent children clung to me like an odour.

"The dolls belong to Mother, but I can't account for how they arrived at their new homes."

Poor Mother was grilled next. Due to her precarious health, the police had come directly to our home. I wasn't allowed to be there while she was questioned. It had been two days since she'd been released from the hospital, and I was too nervous to leave her alone for long stretches of time, so I seized the opportunity to drive to the grocery store to pick up a few necessities. When I returned, Mother had already retired. Every light in the house was off. Grateful, I descended into the basement to turn on my computer and find some torture and peace.

It wasn't until I retrieved the morning paper that I learned the police had concluded their investigation. Mother had apparently confessed to them about depositing the dolls on the doorsteps of neighbourhood girls.

"I thought it was a nice thing I was doing," she was quoted as saying in the newspaper. "I was just giving them presents."

I didn't understand how this was possible. She'd barely been out of my sight these last few weeks. I would ask her after breakfast. But when I brought her coffee and peanut butter on toast, she didn't wake up.

*

I have a theory and it is this: the first museums in the world came into being because a devoted child didn't have the heart to purge his or her parents' belongings.

It was like living in a mausoleum, being here in this house without her. So quiet. Unbearably still. But my girls kept me company. I only emerged from the basement to sleep or prepare simple meals.

When I ran out of money, I realized having an estate sale was my only option. I had no practical use for a thousand precious paperweights, but maybe somebody like Mother would fully appreciate this tacky treasure trove.

I'd keep a few things, of course. The dolls, some old Christmas ornaments, the Harlequin bookend eyesores. I would box these up for safekeeping.

When I retrieve the bookends, armed with a roll of bubble wrap, a piece of paper flutters to the ground. It's an image of perfect little flesh-and-blood Rebecca, naked and cross-legged on a decaying parquet floor. She stares at me accusingly with beautiful, hollow eyes.

On the back of the printout, a yellow Post-it Note with a spurt of Mother's handwriting: "Try not to be what you are," it reads. "For me, Glenny. For me."

It hit me like a cannon of grief and nausea. Mother hadn't deposited the dolls around the neighbourhood. The Girl Scouts had. They had stolen as many dolls as would fit in their knapsacks and redistributed them to the kids in the neighbourhood.

They must have felt like virtuous little Robin Hoods, stealing from the rich and stupid and giving to the tiny and worthy.

But Mother hadn't known about the Girl Scouts. I hadn't mentioned them. She must have thought I was the doll thief. She knew what I was and yet, she was protecting me. She was trying to protect her monster of a son from jail, so she lied and said she thought she was doing a nice thing, giving those dolls to all of those little girls.

"Try not to be what you are. For me . . ."

I stare at the note for what feels like days until the doorbell rings. I crumple up the note and stick it in my back pocket, ushering in the grey-haired estate sale rep, trim and tidy in a blue suit.

"Before I start numbering, is this everything?" she asks me.

"There's one more thing," I say. I haul the computer up from the basement, its various cords hanging limply like zapped tentacles.

"Mother had a thing for eBay," I tell her. "Me, I'm done grad school, so I don't use it much anymore."

"No one's ever interested in old electronics," says the rep. "Donate it to a local school."

"Good idea," I say. "I'll do that."

The next morning, I drove the computer and remaining porcelain dolls to the city dump. I watched our tiny girls shrink and disappear in the rear-view mirror as I drove back to an emptied house.

Controlled Burn

WHEN I GOT UP FROM MY NAP, THE PARK WAS ON FIRE.

"I'd never heard her scream before," Mother said, pausing for a quick sip of pink lemonade. "Not even as a baby. She was always quiet, always smiling. My sweet little jelly roll!"

Mother was selling it as a funny story to impress my uncles and their girlfriends, Stephanie and Pilar. Both were skinny and freckled and tanned, with long brown hair and impossibly small breasts. I was fascinated by their compact golden bodies, perpetually clad in crocheted bikini tops and terry cloth short-shorts. What must it feel like to take up so little space?

"Naturally, I was terrified," she went on. "Lily screaming bloody murder like that, Lord! I thought there must be an intruder in the house!"

I had been five or six and home sick from school. A fever. The doctor said I needed rest and fluids. My bedroom was in the converted attic, my sisters having claimed the other bedrooms in the house by right of birth order. I woke up, turned my head to face the window and saw the smoke and fire through my perch of a window overlooking Parkside Drive. I remember the smoke and I remember screaming, too. I was young, but I was old enough to know what fire was capable of doing to me.

The park was not, in fact, on fire. What I saw was just the annual springtime prescribed burns in High Park. Controlled burns, that's what they call them. Leaves and twigs intentionally ignited by the City of Toronto to help preserve a specific species of tree.

"To this day, she won't even let us light her birthday candles. We have to buy Glow Sticks from Kmart!"

There was an explosion of adult laughter. I pretended to be fascinated by my cuticles.

"Places, everyone!" Lesia's slide whistle signalled the start of the show.

I took my rightful place on the sidelines while Lesia executed an elegant row of cartwheels. Every time she flipped her white sapling legs over and up, her honey-blonde bob delicately grazed the burnt yellow grass of our backyard. There had been a long drought that summer and we weren't supposed to water the lawn. Leah's cartwheels weren't nearly as perfect, but she saved her act by pumping out a series of tight somersaults in quick little bursts, arms and legs pretzelling, her small body a fleshy, kinetic cannonball.

Lesia and Leah dressed alike. They looked alike, too. Whenever people asked if they were twins, they always said "yes" in unison, even though Lesia was a year older.

I am their sister, too. But Lesia and Leah are more like sisters. Like them, I have blonde hair and brown eyes. That's where the similarities end. Lesia always used to wear a broken half-heart necklace that read *Best*. Around Leah's neck, a half-heart that read *Friends*. They saved up for those necklaces. They bought them with their own money.

I could never make my unwieldy body bend and roll in the same ways as my older sisters. The one time Lesia forced me to try a somersault, I split my favourite jeans and hurt my neck. I never tried again after that.

At my annual checkup just before my ninth birthday, I saw my doctor write something next to a number on my chart after weighing me. He looked over at me and smiled kindly.

"Would you mind sending your mother in, Lily?" he said. "I need to have a special meeting with her."

They weren't in there for very long. I heard a bit of my mother's voice yelling and then she came out and told me to get my coat.

"That idiot doctor doesn't know what the hell he's talking about," Mom said in the elevator. She crouched to my height and held my face. "You're perfect. You're my baby girl and you're perfect. Okay?"

On the car ride home, we picked up McDonald's drive-through. I got a Happy Meal. I remember violently plunging a straw into the foil-topped lid of my apple juice, pretending it was someone's larynx. I haven't been to that doctor or any doctor since.

For the show, Lesia had given me the title of stage manager. I wanted to cry and Lesia could tell, so she said that mine was also a very important job. It meant that I would get to introduce the performers ("Leah the Tumblin' Wonderkid and Lesia the *Extremely Great!*"). I'd even get to bow and curtsy with them at the end of the show.

Our parents and our uncles and the girlfriends clapped and cheered from their blue-and-white lawn chairs. I was hot and sweaty and my cheeks felt feverish. I wiped beads of sweat from my upper lip with the back of a chubby wrist and asked my parents if I could be excused.

"But we haven't even eaten yet!" Mother protested.

"I feel overheated!"

"Just let her go," said my father. Then more quietly, "You know as well as I do, she can afford to skip a meal or two."

I escaped into the solitary coolness of our basement to watch TV and eat salt and vinegar chips.

That night, I dreamt the park really was on fire and my parents, sisters, uncles and the girlfriends were all burning along with it. I watched them from a safe distance, eating salt and vinegar chips in a blue-and-white lawn chair. When I woke up, I felt remarkably calm.

*

I was knuckle-deep in a bin of sour jujubes when I first met Pete. Or rather, when Pete first hunted me down. Guys like Pete are divining rods for girls like me.

"Truly charmed, sweet thing," Pete said and I giggled, mostly because I was caught off guard. I wasn't accustomed to male attention. Also, Sweet Thing was the name of the candy shop we were in. I thought that was very clever of him.

Pete was a giant of a man. At first, I thought he was standing on stilts. He was as dramatically slim as I was heavy and I could tell he was a lot older than me because his neatly groomed goatee had streaks of silver in it. He wore a bowler hat and a three-piece suit that made him look like a circus ringmaster or a particularly elegant pimp. Pete's nose was large and porous and the highly pronounced Adam's apple that jutted out of his neck reminded me of a turkey's wattle. I found him to be devastatingly handsome.

"What's your name? Wait! Let me guess let me guess let me guess," he said, barely pausing between words. Syllables and consonants crowded his mouth like teeth.

"With those resplendent golden tresses of yours, you must be an Emma."

"Wrong."

"The lovely Josephine, I presume?"

"Nope!"

"Ah," he said, as though my true identity had slowly come into focus. "It is an absolute pleasure to meet you, Cunégonde!"

I giggled again, just as I expect he expected I might. He smiled when I told him it was Lily.

"The most beautiful and delicate of flowers," he said solemnly. "I should have known."

From his shirt sleeve, he produced a red rose and a black rectangle of gleaming paper stock, embossed with a small white rabbit.

"My business card, Mademoiselle," he said. "Contact information is on the back, in case you ever find yourself in need of a magician for a birthday party or corporate event, wedding or bar mitzvah."

"Thank you."

"Forgive me, should I have addressed you as Madame?" he asked and I shook my head. "A beauty like you, still unspoken for?" He raised a bushy black eyebrow. "The men in this city are quite insane."

I evaded his follow-up question about my age by looking away and coyly responding I was old enough to know better. I was, in fact, not old enough to know anything much at all. I was sixteen and a half when I met Pete, although that half-year mattered about as much in this situation as any given half-inch on his six foot seven frame.

Pete suddenly reached out to touch my face. I didn't recoil, even as I felt an odd sensation against my neck. From my left ear, he had produced a Walnut Whip, wrapped in crinkly blue metallic foil.

"Ever try one of these?" he asked and I shook my head. "They're imported. And a bit nutty, just like me." He unwrapped it and nudged it into my mouth. It was maybe the best chocolate I had ever tasted. A curvy miniature mountain cast in chocolate, crowned with a cloud of walnut. On the inside, I discovered dewy marshmallow softness that I wasn't expecting.

"You like?" His eyes locked onto mine and I nodded.

That was when Pete suggested I go for a walk in the park with him. Only he didn't use the word *walk*. Pete said *promenade*.

His enormous hand latched onto my warm, sweaty one as securely as a magnet. *Holyshitholyshit.* I felt a belly-flutter of worry. My parents lived nearby; what if they saw me holding hands with a strange older man? No no no, they wouldn't be home for another couple of hours. But Lesia and Leah? And what if anybody who knew any of them saw us? I had always been taught to never ever talk to strangers, and here I was holding hands and going on romantic "promenades" with one.

Despite my worry, I felt a small thrill at the potential of being seen, being noticed. Finally. Finally. I had waited my whole life to be looked at the way Pete was looking at me right now.

I was completely invisible at my high school. I'd read awful stories about the mistreatment and bullying that some fat girls faced at their schools, but I had suffered none of that. I sat in plastic-backed orange chairs at the backs of classrooms and took notes on textbooks balanced on my lap because I couldn't fit behind the standard desks. I spent my lunch hours peacefully drawing anthropomorphic cats in notebooks with a sweet Japanese exchange student who barely spoke a word of English, although she did say "So cute!" a great deal. No one ever said anything cruel to me, but nobody ever said hello, either. I was smart and got good grades, but my teachers rarely called on me to participate. I was an immense and uncomfortable ghost, taking it all in but never a full participant in the proceedings. Perhaps people felt they were doing me a kindness by negating my physical presence instead of drawing any sort of attention to me. No one wanted me to notice their disgust, so they pretended to not notice me at all.

That winter had been mercifully mild and April had been so unseasonably warm that the cherry trees were blooming prematurely. Overnight frost could have easily killed them. They were that delicate. Drunk on Pete's attentions, I looked up at the fragile pink blossoms in wonder and gratitude. They reflected my youth and beauty back at me.

We approached the Adventure playground. It was completely empty.

"I spent years studying Harry Houdini," Pete said, weaving his fingers between the monkey bars. "The art of escape. My body type made Houdini's tricks particularly challenging, you understand. So I specialized. Found my niche. Now, I mostly make things appear ... and disappear."

From my right ear, Pete produced a Ring Pop. He popped it out of the foil casing and fell to one knee on the dusty gravel. We were eye to eye. Equals.

"Marry me."

I laughed and covered my face with my hands.

"I'm serious," he said, and I looked at him and felt that he was. He slipped the ring onto the fourth finger of my left hand and slid it halfway down; that was as far as it could go. As I brought it to my lips, I admired how the green sugar jewel glinted in the warm spring sunlight. It was as radiant as any emerald.

Pete pointed out the plumes of smoke and my heart stopped. Instead of leaving the park at my urging, he grabbed my wrist and led me toward the source. The main path of the park was cordoned off with yellow caution tape, but Pete effortlessly stepped over it and held it down for me to do the same.

"Just act like you own the place," he whispered, leading me down the path.

Neither of us was particularly hard to miss, so it wasn't long before a park worker yelled at us through his mask to "exit the area immediately." But not before my eyes took in the burning embers all around us; red and orange and a filthy, ashen grey. I stood frozen, feeling the radiant heat on my cheeks, my arms. I coughed woodsmoke from my lungs, earthy and sweet.

"You there! Get the hell away from here!" yelled another, less outwardly professional park worker. Pete tipped his hat while bowing dramatically, took my hand again and quickly led me away the three or four blocks to his house.

"There's a controlled burn like that every year," I told Pete as he unlocked the front door to his house with a heavy old antique key. I was out of breath. So exhilarated from our little adventure, I hadn't even thought about where we were heading.

"I used to set fire to little things when I was a kid," Pete said, as the door swung open. "Bits of tissue, grocery store receipts, anthills. That sort of thing."

"I'm a little bit afraid of fire," I admitted.

He closed the door behind us and reached for my face as I smiled and closed my eyes, wondering what sort of candy he would pull out of my ear next.

That's when his tongue appeared in my mouth.

*

I had been secretly dating Pete for about a month when my parents sat me down.

"We need to talk," said my father. Mother's mouth was a thin, pinched line.

The room spun out of control and my brain went into overdrive. Oh god. They knew! How could they have ever found out? We'd been so careful! I hadn't told anyone except my friend Yuki and I wasn't entirely confident she knew enough English to understand what I was even talking about (although she encouraged me endlessly with a string of "So cutes!").

"Your mother and I have decided to enrol you in a fitness camp this summer," Dad said.

"It's in the Muskokas," chirped Mother. "Not too far away from home and apparently quite nice! They even have a day when the families can come up and do a colour war!"

I started to cry. The relief that they didn't know about Pete was enormous. The thought of being away from him for an entire summer was gut-twisting anguish. I was almost a woman who was almost in love, but I still had no control over my life. My body heaved out uncontrollable sobs.

"Oh! My poor baby!" said Mother. Suddenly, she was crying along with me.

"We'll write you as often as we can," my father offered weakly.

"Let's have some dinner, hmm?" suggested Mother. "I picked up all of your favourites, Jelly Roll! Baby back ribs, creamy potato salad and strawberry cheesecake for dessert!"

Jack Sprat could eat no fat,
His wife could eat no lean;
And so between the two of them,
They licked the platter clean.

I was too embarrassed to tell Pete the real reason I was being sent away. Instead, I told him that I was working as a camp counsellor because I needed a more robust employment history for my university applications next year. He told me he understood. He told me he'd write every day.

Fitness camp was a euphemism, of course, but I made the best of the fat farm. The other girls in my cabin were awesome and wanted to hang out all the time. We went to our paltry meals together, shared notes after nutrition class, collapsed after aerobics classes and kept pace together during gruelling group hikes in the woods. Eventually, we collectively picked up smoking to kill our appetites – it just made everything easier if you weren't hungry all the time. We screamed along to "Plump" from Hole's new album *Live Through This*; dyed each other's hair green, purple and red with sugar-free drink crystals and bingo dabbers; snuck out at night to drink and smoke contraband in the shadows; skinny-dipped in the moon-light without fear or shame. Our daylight hours were made up of aerobics and torture but we took refuge in the fact that we were an ironclad infantry; a chubby cabal of eye-rolling, chain-smoking rebels. We would sweat together, bleed together, starve together, drink together, stick together. We called ourselves the BWFs (Babes With Fattitude) and we would, we were certain, live through this.

A letter from Pete arrived just about every day, as promised. The first one looked like a blank sheet of paper, but I knew better. Invisible ink. I held our communal lighter under it and revealed Pete's chicken scratch handwriting and almost total dismissal of punctuation.

My cabin asked me to read my letters from my boyfriend out loud. They had me repeat the sexy bits and shrieked, scandalized. The only other person in the cabin who had been kissed was Diana, but that really didn't count because it was on a dare and he was her second cousin. In an early letter, Pete begged for photos of me. One of the girls had brought her Polaroid camera for the summer and we snuck off at mealtime to cheekily snap a few topless ones of me on the dock, sunning myself like a sensual seal.

"You're a gem of a jewel of a pearl of a girl," he would sign off on all of his letters. "xoxo, Pete."

He would often enclose candy and chocolates in his care packages, but I would slide them into the space under a loose floorboard in our cabin or else trade them on the camp's black market for extra cigarettes and tampons with applicators. I didn't want or need the extra sugar. Smoking took the cravings away. The weight was falling off of me. Once the headaches subsided, it started happening all at once. I was committing biological arson, burning millions of small fires on a cellular level. I had become a magician of my own body; I was making my great mass disappear.

By midsummer, the changes were dramatic. I was far from thin, but I was practically unrecognizable from the first day of camp. My size 4X jeans hung off my body. My double chin was single again. At first, these physical changes had felt like a triumph, but I now felt strangely disconnected from my own body. It didn't feel like it belonged to me at all anymore. It belonged to some other person. Some starving, faraway girl who somehow got by on 850 calories a day and who was frighteningly adept at taking her brain away during interval training. I was like one of those beautiful magician's assistants being sawed in half in the Box of Mystery – I could wiggle my toes but I wasn't convinced they were even attached to me. Looking at myself in the mirror felt just as strange – who *was* this person? This stranger with the suddenly emergent cheekbones, toned upper arms and bright, forced smile? Whenever I felt sort of blue about it, I started thinking about September and how amazed and happy Pete would be to see me looking like this. People in my classes would finally start to get to know me in my final year. Teachers would call out my name and ask for my thoughts on the sonnets of Shakespeare and John Donne. I'd answer them as a woman who was no stranger to acts of love.

It had been a while since I'd sent Pete a photo. He had been begging and begging, so I posed for another Polaroid photo shoot. The August sun seared the sky as I posed fully nude and confident in my more socially acceptable beauty. Anointed in coconut-scented tanning oil, I knew how luminous I must have looked. The stranger I had become was the golden goddess of Cabin 6B; a Rubenesque sculpture revealed by aggressively chipping away at a monolithic slab of fat. All it took were coffee and cigarettes, bear crawls and burpees.

I enclosed my latest Polaroid in a letter so scandalous that I'd actually blushed while writing it. Trembling, I licked the stamps and dropped it in the mail. Then, I waited.

No response.

I asked the camp director for special access to the one telephone on-site.

"Is it an emergency?" he asked, bored.

"I mean, not exactly."

"Then it can wait until you get back home, can't it?"

When my parents came to collect me on Labour Day, they praised me for the weight that I had lost, but I was quiet and distracted. Had my letter gotten lost in the mail? And even if it had, why had Pete stopped writing so abruptly? Had there been an accident? Was he hurt?

When I finally dialled the number I knew off by heart, I got his answering machine. I left three messages on it on my first night back.

Call me please read the note I stuffed into his mail slot when he didn't answer his door for the fifth time. The note was on stationery with my name on it, so there was no mistaking the sender. When I peeked through the mail slot, I noticed that his mail was not piling up on the floor. There were no bills, no flyers, no collection of letters from a heartbroken girl. It was all being collected by its intended recipient. I felt a wave of relief, followed by anger, followed by despair. Pete was not missing or dead. Pete was very much alive. He had just made himself disappear.

It wasn't until early November that I saw him again. I was biking in High Park after school and saw him looking at the peacocks in the zoo with a short blonde girl easily twice my size. Their backs were turned to me, but I knew right away it was him. A guy like Pete is hard to miss. I dismounted, laid my bike on the ground and, fumbling with my wallet, approached them.

"Excuse me." I was amazed by how calm I sounded. *Just act like you own the place.*

Pete and the girl both turned around.

"You dropped something," I said, offering him his old business card back.

"Oh, thank you so much!" said the girl. I didn't even look at her. I needed her to exist on the periphery, if she had to exist at all. An immense and uncomfortable ghost.

"Oh, I have a million of those," Pete said. If he recognized me, he didn't let on. "Please, just keep it for yourself."

"He's a wonderful magician," said the girl. "Available for weddings and bar mitzvahs."

I nodded lightly, pocketed the card and rode off.

Bits of tissue, grocery store receipts, anthills. That sort of thing.

I had a fancy metallic lighter in my pocket. My summer camp smoking habit had remained. When you want something less, it makes everything so much easier. Refined sugar. Any food at all. A certain man. I remembered there were some receipts in my wallet. Crisp and perfect kindling.

I biked to Pete's house and gingerly fed flaming objects through his mail slot, one at a time. His business card, creased with wear, combusted quickly and easily.

I watched as flames licked at the bottom of his front door. As if they were feeding on the oxygen of my rage, the flames grew higher and higher, igniting his carpet and lapping at the legs of his small wooden foyer chair. I biked away, one thousand infernos burning the sky black in my head, Courtney Love screeching through my Discman.

When I got home, I thought I heard a scared little girl screaming somewhere in the distance, but it was too far away to tell for sure.

Ark

"I NEED A MAN WHO WILL KISS ME LIKE HE'S ABOUT to be sent to the firing squad," Shelby declared between drags of her cigarette. "What kind of man are you looking for, Julia?"

"I dunno." I picked at my scabs. "Somebody nice, I guess." We'd been sitting on the football bleachers of our high school field, watching the junior boys on their warm-up run. They were a small army made up of sharp elbows and concave chests, rosy cheeks blemished by freckles and acne. Shelby insisted they were handsome.

I looked over at her, admiring her translucent skin and dark, Mary Quant–inspired bob haircut. A delicate blue vein pulsed at her temple.

Shelby had spent that summer living in France with her aunt and uncle. She had developed an expansive vocabulary and a languorous, world-weary attitude.

And also breasts.

I noticed all the boys were noticing her now.

With my flat chest, chipmunk cheeks and mousy brown hair that always fell into my eyes, I remained blessedly invisible. To boys. To girls. To teachers. To everyone but Shelby.

The mid-September air that day was as oppressively hot as it was in mid-August. Remnants of summer remained. Near my left toe, a bottle cap caught the late afternoon sunlight in such a way that I remember thinking it was a very large, very still blue beetle.

When the boys started doing jumping jacks after their laps, I tried not to laugh. They looked, to me, like sweaty marionettes; two dozen pale, leaping Howdy Doodys. Shelby applauded and let out a flirtatious whoop.

"Tommy looks a little like Burt Lancaster, don't you think?"

I squinted hard. I couldn't see the resemblance at all, but I said, "A bit," before getting back to picking the scab on my knee. It bled around the edges, but it itched so much.

"Darling, don't pick at your scabs!" Shelby slapped my wrist. *"C'est vraiment grossier!"*

I didn't even try to keep up with her French. I only knew *bonjour* and *au revoir* and *pomme* and the French word for seal, but only because it sounds like something rude.

I stopped picking my knee scabs and headed straight for my cuticles. Shelby sighed like an indulgent mother. "Whatever will we do with you?"

I didn't know who else she meant, because we were the only ones there.

When practice was over, Tommy waved in our direction. Shelby waved back. He barrelled over to us like an oversized Saint Bernard, grinning and glistening.

"Hiya, Shelby," he said.

"Thomas, you dear thing!" She acknowledged him with a demure double cheek kiss and I winced at the sight of her cool cheek colliding with his pockmarked, sweaty jowl. "Aren't you forgetting someone?"

"Hey, Julia. Good summer?"

I mustered up the necessary levels of enthusiasm to respond with a "Yeah!" Since Tommy was something of a dolt, I didn't want to confuse him by using language that was overly complex.

Shelby and Tommy moved down the bench and chatted for a while. She'd purr excited run-on sentences and he would answer in sheepish monosyllables. I made no effort to participate or even eavesdrop. I was too busy weaving some dandelions into a chain – a complicated task that demanded my full attention.

"We're leaving," Shelby announced. I felt relief wash over me until I saw Shelby and Tommy's hands were interlocked. "Get home safe, *ma chérie.*" It sounded, to me, like a taunt.

"I made you a bracelet," I said, extending thin arms toward her. Shelby smiled and held out the hand that wasn't all tangled up in Tommy's paw.

*

Underneath the old stone footbridge. That was our hiding place. Every Wednesday evening last year, when our mothers thought we were at choir practice, we would make our way there. Sometimes we'd arrive together. Sometimes separately.

"There used to be water here," I told her once. "When I was very little, we would play in this creek. We'd catch tadpoles sometimes. But it's all dried up now."

"I can still feel it," Shelby whispered.

"Feel what?"

"The memory of water."

Shelby brought a flashlight sometimes so we could see well enough to read chapters of *Lady Chatterley's Lover* to each other and string single buttons onto lengths of thread. She would show me how to tie it and then pull the thread taut taut taut so that the button would vibrate and spin and hum in mid-air. We pretended they were magical fleas at a flea circus and we were the ringmasters. For the grand finale, we would touch the vibrating strings to our tongues and laugh until we collapsed.

We had a secret: The footbridge was not really a footbridge. It was actually a bomb shelter in disguise. Invisible glass surrounded us. Nobody knew it was a bomb shelter except for us.

One day, we imagined the bomb came. And when we re-entered the outside world, everybody was dead. Our mothers. Our fathers. Our teachers. Shelby's pet rabbit, Ginger. An H-bomb would drop while we were innocently playing gin rummy and we wouldn't hear a thing. Not a whisper. Not a scream.

"It'd be just like that episode of *The Twilight Zone*," Shelby said. She lowered her voice and over-enunciated in an attempt to emulate Rod Serling: *"Witness Mr. Henry Bemis . . . a charter member in the fraternity of dreamers."* I hadn't seen that one. She told me if a bomb dropped, we would have all the time in the world to read books to one another, just as long as our glasses didn't break. She seemed relieved to hear that I had perfect 20/20 vision.

Shelby was always so beautiful in the half-darkness. In the half-darkness, so was I.

I can't really remember how it started.

No. That's a lie.

She had been very quiet one afternoon. I was worried that she was upset with me about something. She told me that she had sort of Frenched a boy at overnight camp when she was twelve but hadn't done anything with anyone since. She asked if I had ever been kissed and I shook my head no. She said that I could practise for the real thing with her, if I wanted.

Everything went perfectly still. It was as if the big one really had happened and we were just two tiny specks of dust floating alone in the universe. I couldn't process anything except Shelby's unsteady breathing, the smell of the White Shoulders perfume she periodically stole from her mother and the sound of running water, but there was no water anywhere near that bridge, so maybe I was just imagining it.

*

Shelby wasn't at school the day after we watched the boys' football practice. During attendance, Mrs. Macpherson announced, "Shelby is excused." After class, I asked and she told me that Shelby's mother had called the school that morning to say that Shelby wasn't feeling well.

Even though it was starting to rain, I hopped on my bike at lunch and rode to Shelby's house. I was going to take her the orange that my mother had packed in my lunch for the vitamin C. I decided that I would give Shelby's mother a little break from playing nurse. I would read Keats and Shelley and Dickinson aloud to Shelby and feed her chips of ice with a spoon and smooth her soft, dark hair away from her feverish forehead. And she would feel better. Maybe she would even teach me some French words. She'd be so grateful that she had a friend like me.

"She's upstairs resting, hon," Shelby's mother said, barely looking up from her rapid-fire knitting. Knit one, purl one. Green and yellow yarn.

I walked up the stairs and quietly entered Shelby's bed-room. She was facing the window, her body curled up tightly, like a snail's shell. Her breathing was steady and rhythmic. Inhale, exhale. Silence in between.

I sat on the corner of her bed.

"Hi," I said.

"I brought you an orange," I said.

She didn't say a word.

I remember thinking she must really be sick if she didn't feel like talking.

I began to slowly unravel the orange so the skin stayed all in one piece – something I learned from an old camp counsellor. I laid the orange peel down in front of her face, hoping my trick would make her laugh.

Shelby didn't speak and she didn't move. She continued breathing steadily, but I could tell she was awake. I laid my hand on her cool, exposed shoulder and started to hum a French lullaby she had taught me. I wanted to sing it out loud properly for her, but I didn't know most of the words. *Ma chandelle est morte. Ma chandelle est morte. Ma chandelle est morte. Je n'ai plus.*

Thunder rumbled on the horizon and Shelby's breathing got less steady. I thought she was laughing at me for not knowing the words or for singing off-key until I realized she was crying. I'd never heard her cry like that. I'd never heard her cry at all. Strong, stubborn, beautiful Shelby. My hand was still on her shoulder. I got to thinking about electrical circuits in science class and how I didn't ever want our circuit to break so I was never going to take my hand off her shoulder. I would keep it there forever – or until I ran out of lullabies. I started to hum another one.

Shelby suddenly turned her beautiful, swollen face toward me.

"It's not like in the movies," she said. "It's nothing like the books say."

Lightning. Thunder. Another loud noise, like a wooden structure splitting. Cracking. Creaking. The room tilted. Shelby's bedroom was filling up with water. Cold water. Dark. It crept up so fast. It poured through the windows. It bled in through the doorway. It dripped through pores in the ceiling. Shelby's bedside lamp sparked and the bulb popped like a champagne cork. Her bed began to float. The sound of rushing water filled my head, but instead of the ghostly rustle of a creek that had since dried up into nothing, the whole of the ocean surrounded us now. We clung onto each other for dear life. I could hear the waves collapsing around our two warm bodies, waves that pushed and pulled sand and debris in its wake, accompanied by a greedy undertow that clutched onto anything and everything it could carry along with it.

Something to Cry About

For Mary Margaret O'Hara

This is a survival guide for you and your family. It contains information on what to do before, during and after a nuclear attack. Read it with care as it could greatly increase your chances of survival.

THERE ARE ONE HUNDRED AND THIRTY-TWO THOU-sand, four hundred and eighty-eight tiles on this floor. I know because I counted them. I tapped each one with the tip of my precision compass to ensure absolute accuracy. And then I counted them all over again, just to make sure. It took me three tries. I lost count twice because Dad started ragging on me to stop. I honestly didn't mind starting over, though. We have a lot of time to count things down here. There isn't much else to do.

So something happened. Something bad. Dad says there was an explosion. But not just any explosion. It was a nuclear explosion. (Mahkizmo didn't even have anything to do with it, though.) It was caused by people who live far away. Very bad people across the sea shooting missiles at us. The explosion happened just after 3:00 a.m. somewhere in New York State. We don't live in New York State, but Dad says it's not too far away from us. Not too far away from us at all.

The thing about nuclear explosions is that they're poisonous. Like, there's this poison that gets released – kind of like a poisonous gas but not – and the poison can travel really far. It can travel fast, too. Faster than I can run. Probably not faster than The Flash, though. Nothing and no one's faster than The Flash. Not even cheetahs. Not even light. Poison released after a nuclear explosion is called fallout. Dad says our basement shelter will protect us from the fallout. Dad says he won't ever let anything bad happen to his family. Dad says he has everything under control.

Last Saturday, Dad woke us up in the middle of the night.

"Get dressed," he said. I thought I was in trouble. He put his hand on my forehead like Mom does whenever I have a fever.

"Mmnnphwhaa?"

"This is not a drill," he said. "It's time."

I said, "Time for what?" But he was already gone, knocking on Ginny's door.

"Take only what you need," I heard him tell her. "Pack only what is absolutely essential."

I was already dressed. I like to sleep in my clothes sometimes. I slid out of bed and filled my backpack with as many comic books as I could grab. I used a flashlight because the power was out. I took a whole pile of *Fantastic Four*s, plus a couple of *Richie Rich* and *Archie* digests for Ginny, in case she forgot to bring hers. I also brought along a calculus textbook I got from the library, my geometry set, some mechanical pencils and the miniature abacus Grandma got me for Christmas. Oh, and some clean socks and underwear.

"Always wear clean underwear," Dad always says. When I asked Mom what Dad meant by that, she said that we should always wear clean underwear in case we have to go to the hospital. This always confused me. Would the doctors not help me if my underwear was dirty?

"Jim, what's going on?" Mom's voice was shaky and my legs were shaky, like we were both standing in the middle of an earthquake. I've never been in an earthquake, but I've read about them. Mom says she felt one once when she was in California, before she met Dad, but it was only a 3.9 on the Richter scale, which isn't such a big deal.

"Put these on," said Dad, handing each of us a mask I'd only ever seen on TV. They made us look like insects. No, wait, they made us look like robots! They made us look like H.E.R.B.I.E. in the *Fantastic Four*.

"Manipulators extend!" I said in my very best robot voice.

"Be quiet, Marcus. Breathe normally, everyone. Got it?"

We breathed normally.

"Follow me," said Dad. "Quickly, now. Don't dawdle!"

We followed him. Quickly. We didn't dawdle.

"Manipulators extend," I said, but nobody heard.

Plan today for what you would have to do in order to survive a nuclear attack. The plans you make could also ensure survival of you and your family in the event of a local natural emergency. There is a checklist at the end of this pamphlet to help you plan logically.

Down here in Subterranea, I have counted fifty-six cans of creamed corn; forty cans of corned beef; twenty-seven cans each of kidney beans, whole new potatoes, string beans, butter beans, baked beans, canned peaches and tomato soup; and seventy-two tins of sardines packed in oil. There are seventeen tins of juice: six apple, six grapefruit, one orange and four tomato. There are twelve boxes of cereal: six are Cheerios, four are Shreddies and two are Shredded Wheat. I hate Shredded Wheat. It tastes like cardboard. No, I've never actually eaten cardboard but I've eaten Shredded Wheat, so I know what I'm talking about. There are also eleven boxes of instant rice, thirteen bottles of red wine, twelve tins of –

"Marcus, that's enough," says Dad.

"But I'm taking inventory of our food!"

"Why don't you do something else?" says Dad.

There are two hundred and twenty-five emergency candles – in forty-five packages of five. Four gas masks. Three 100-litre water storage tanks. I have previously counted and noted sixty-four rolls of single-ply toilet paper, a box of one hundred blue nitrile (surgical) gloves, two first aid kits, five flashlights, one box of flares, five boxes of strike anywhere matches, six blankets, ten rolls of duct tape, four packages of moist towelettes, three fire extinguishers, two cans of kerosene, one bungee cord –

"And a partridge in a pear tree," says Ginny. She flicks a pink snap barrette at my head.

"Marcus," says Dad, a little louder than last time.

"What?"

"I already told you, son. Do something else."

"But I am!" I say. "I'm taking inventory of the non-food items."

"Holy smokes, Marcus!" says Ginny. "Can't you shut up for even like *five minutes?*"

"I am simply *counting*," I breathe. There are miniature nuclear explosions in my brain. Fallout everywhere. I feel poisoned. I feel poisonous.

"Ginny, don't tell your brother to shut up," says Mom from the cot in the corner. "Leave Marcus alone, Jim. He finds numbers smooooothing." Mom is wearing her old pink bathrobe and drinking out of a mug that says *Thank God It's Friday*. Her mouth is the colour of Welch's grape juice.

"Jesus Christ, Donna," says Dad. "It's not even noon yet."

"It's noon somewherrrrrre," sings Mom. "Over the rainbow!"

"I can *too* shut up for five minutes," I say. I start counting to three hundred in my head. That's sixty seconds times five, which is five minutes. Eight. Nine. Ten.

"What in the hell does it matter what time it is anymore?" Mom's voice is loud and she sounds like she's about to cry. "What in the hell does anything matter?" Mom stands and drops the mug she's holding, maybe by accident but also maybe not. It shatters and I smell the sour smell of definitely not grape juice. I'll have to count the pieces later, before Mom cleans it up, which she will. Maybe she'll do that tomorrow. She will clean it up when she is feeling less upset, because nobody else will. It's a mother's job to clean things. Everyone knows that.

Thirty-nine. Forty. Almost one whole minute of me shutting up.

Dad has grabbed Mom by the shoulders and is shaking her. Mom is really crying now.

I love my little mommy. She used to sing me lullabies and is such a nice singer. She used to act in musicals, did you know that? She always played the biggest and best roles because she is so pretty and such a nice singer. Maria in *West Side Story*. Kim in *Bye Bye Birdie*. Julie in *Carousel*. She showed me all of the playbills once. She acted in them before I was born. Mom is really so beautiful. Even when there are bruises on her face. Even when she cries.

Don't cry. Don't cry. Hold it together. Be a man.

Forty-seven. Forty-eight.

Whether you choose to evacuate or take shelter locally, you should have a roadmap with you. You can then relate the information about areas under fallout, which you would hear about on the radio, to your actual location. Toys, games, books for your children would help to occupy their time. Your battery-powered radio will keep you in contact with the outside world.

Ginny's iron has just landed on my hotel on Baltic Avenue.

"Four hundred and fifty buckaroonies," I tell her. "Pay up, miss."

"I'm shaking in my boots," says Ginny. "Whatever, Marcus. It's only stupid Baltic Avenue anyway. It's the most welfare property ever."

"Pay up, please," I say.

Ginny makes a farting noise with her mouth and counts out a rainbow of Monopoly money.

"There!" she says. "Happy?"

I nod and twirl the ends of my pretend millionaire's moustache.

Ginny makes another farting noise and flips over the Monopoly board.

"Hey!" I feel every drop of blood in my face drain into my belly.

"Gross, there was a centipede on it," Ginny says. "Guess we have to start all over again."

"But I was winning!" I start to cry.

"Oh grow up, you big baby! I don't play games with babies." Ginny walks away and opens up an *Archie* comic book.

Mom and Dad aren't yelling at us because they aren't paying attention to us. They're talking in low voices. I can hear them in bits and pieces, between sniffles.

"My mother," says Mom. "No way she could have . . . It's gone now. Everything."

"Not all bad."

"How could you say that?"

"I guess your good friend Richard is gone, too." Dad's voice is louder now, and shaky. Dad never shakes. Dad never wavers, quavers. "Won't be bumping into him at the grocery store anytime soon, will you? Going over for a morning coffee to chat and all that."

There is quiet for a while.

"I told you. Was already over. Already done."

"Like I'm supposed to believe that," Dad says. "Once a lying bitch, always a lying bitch."

Mom goes to the washroom and slams the door shut. I hear the lock click, even though Dad tells us we're not supposed to lock the door in case of an emergency.

Dad wanders over to the corner of the room where he keeps the transistor radio. He moves the dials back and forth dramatically while looking at us. He does this every single day, like singing the national anthem or saying the Lord's Prayer. I never hear anything coming out of that radio. Not even static.

Persons who become emotionally disturbed following a disaster should be treated calmly but firmly. They should be kept in small groups, preferably with people they know. They should be encouraged to talk out their problem. If they are not otherwise injured, they should be given something to do. It may be necessary to enlist the aid of another calm person to help restrain

the over-excited person. If a stunned or dazed reaction persists for over six to eight hours this should be reported to a doctor or nurse immediately when one becomes available.

Ginny cried and screamed a lot for the first forty-eight hours or so in Subterranea. She was worried about Grandma and her best friend, Carol. Were they dead? Was everyone dead? What if everybody we knew was dead or dying? How could we not go find them and help them? Would she still get to go to high school in September? What if all of the teachers had already dropped dead from radiation poisoning? Would she never get to be in a high school musical?

I cupped my hands against my ears to try to block out all the noise. I tried to focus on the sounds of the ocean in my hands but she would not stop crying and she would not stop screaming. She even tried to open the door to the main part of the house, but Dad wrestled her to the ground.

"You do not endanger your life like that," Dad screamed into her ear and she yelped. "Do you hear me? Do you understand? You do not endanger our lives like that!"

Then Ginny quieted down and Dad got all quiet and gentle, while still pinning her arms and legs. "Baby, we are safe here. This is a safe, private fortress just for us. For you, your brother, your mother and me. No bad guys are getting in and nobody is getting out. Do you hear me? Do you understand? Tell me you understand."

That's when Ginny exploded into bloody murder screaming, which was not very fun, believe me. Murder bloody murder bloody murder screaming. I never want to hear that sound coming out of my sister or anybody else ever again. Dad put his hand over her mouth but that only made things worse. She gnashed and bit and howled like a trapped animal.

Then I heard someone else start crying. A little kid. I didn't realize it was me until I put my hands to my face and felt the tears.

"Keep that up," Dad glared at me, "and I'll *give* you something to cry about."

Ginny kept screaming. That's when Dad slapped Ginny's face. Hard. Ginny went all quiet and Mom started to sob. I shut my eyes and tried to think of something new to count.

Okay but don't worry – I found something. It was the seconds between Mom's sobs. I counted longer and longer between each time, just like with the pauses between lightning and thunder during a storm as it passes us over and the thunder sounds get farther apart from the lightning and you can finally, finally fall asleep.

It is important to provide your family and yourself with shelter. But what kind of shelter? This is a decision you must make yourself after studying the problem. Study your shelter requirements in the same way that you would accident or fire insurance. Decide upon the degree of protection you want for yourself and your

family. Shelter is your insurance against something you hope will not happen, but if it does, it will give you protection.

Here's what it looks like in our real-life Subterranea: a cold tile floor. There are one hundred and thirty-two thousand, four hundred and eighty-eight tiles, as I've said. They are white and in the shape of hexagons. If you stare at the floor too long, it starts to shimmer and move and make you feel kind of dizzy. The floor is cold, even though it's summertime. We have to wear our shoes at all times because otherwise our feet get cold and dirty and there's no hot water because the hot water tank isn't working.

There are three cots: mine, Ginny's and a bigger cot that Mom and Dad share, which is in the corner of the basement. Dad's made sort of a separate room for their cot by hanging a yellow blanket on our indoor clothesline in front of it, like a curtain.

They leave the curtain open, mostly. Dad is already dressed in the mornings. Mom doesn't usually change out of her robe. Last night, though, they closed the curtain after lights out. I could hear them talking a bit. Whispering. Mom said something like, Are you kidding, what about the kids. She was saying no. No no no no no. Jim, the children, are you kidding me? Dad kept shushing her and saying It's okay, it's okay, it's okay. Then they made noises like grunting and the cot springs made noises like crickets chirping at night.

So maybe you think I'm a stupid baby who doesn't know anything but I'm not. Even though Ginny says that I am a stupid baby like every single day. I've read a lot of books and comics, you know. I've seen a lot of movies and even more TV shows. I know about the things that happen in the nighttime between moms and dads. I'm really glad it only happens at nighttime. I was glad Ginny was asleep so she didn't have to listen to it. I could hear her snoring. Or maybe she was fake snoring.

I am going to tell you about the rest of the basement now.

There is a laundry sink and a washing machine and dryer, but we're not able to use anything that needs electricity. The power has been out since evacuation. I flick the light on and off a few times every day, just to make sure. Dad gets pretty mad at me about that.

There are six sconces built in but we're only allowed to burn candles in four of them at a time. We can use a kerosene lamp if we want to play board games or cards or read, but that's only allowed for two hours out of the day.

There are no windows.

The walls are grey and rough. If I ask for permission first, I can light matches on them. "Poured concrete," says Dad. "Nothing's getting through these walls."

There is a small washroom in the left-hand corner. Inside, there is a flashlight and a neatly printed sign that reads, *If it's yellow, let it mellow. If it's brown, flush it down.* We keep the door closed all the time now, because of the smell.

Cooking in any confined shelter poses problems of fire hazards and potential poisoning by carbon monoxide gas. The choice of a suitable cooker means balancing risk against necessity. Small quantities of liquid may be heated in the shelter space using, for example, a candle-heated coffee warmer of the type often used at the dining table. This will do well for baby foods. More serious cooking requires some form of cooker, and the kerosene wick-type cooker is probably the safest, followed by primus Coleman-type stoves and butane cookers.

"Who's ready for breakfast?" says Dad in a singsong voice, sounding happier and more cheerful than I've heard him sound in a long time. He is stirring a pot of Boston baked beans on the kerosene stove with a wooden spoon.

Ginny groans. "Not baked beans for breakfast again."

"It's important to start the day off with protein," says Dad. "Would you prefer sardines for breakfast?" Ginny makes dramatic gagging noises.

It's my turn to wash the dishes and cutlery in the laundry sink. I hum quietly to myself until Ginny tells me to stop being so annoying. The liquid dish soap is a dark, chemical green. It makes me think of Doctor Doom's cloak. What would my superpower be? Could I defeat Doctor Doom?

"What would happen if we went outside right now?" I ask.

"You don't want to know," says Dad.

"Your skin would turn black and fall off and cockroaches and earwigs would eat your eyes and your dumb face," says Ginny.

"Ginny, that's disgusting!" says Mom.

"Okay but! What if, instead of dying, we got superpowers?" I say. "Like Reed Richards!"

"Who in the hell is Reed Richards?" says Dad.

"Reed Richards is the alter ego of Mister Fantastic," I say. "That was his identity before his spaceship got hit by cosmic radiation and he became a superhero."

"Marcus is like obsessed with the Fantastic Four," says Ginny. "Do you ever listen to a word he says?"

"Who's up for canasta?" says Mom.

That's when Dad's watch alarm goes off.

"Canasta will have to wait," says Dad. "Time for calisthenics."

Ginny moans and groans and makes a big show out of not wanting to do them. I pretend I like them. It's one of the only times Dad isn't on my case or yelling at me, really. I just smile and smile and do all of the motions. Most of the time, I barely even sweat.

So what happens is Dad wakes us all up at 6:00 a.m. by clanging a pot with a wooden spoon. He's already been up for hours he says, and tells us to move our lazy bones. It's so hard for me to wake up in the mornings, but Dad doesn't need an alarm clock or anything. When I ask him why his body automatically gets him up so early, he tells me he's been doing that since he was in the military.

"If we don't exercise every day, our muscles will turn to mush," says Dad. "That includes our brains, which is why we're going to do some crossword puzzles later as our scheduled group activity. Your brain is the most important muscle in your body. When your brain goes, you're just meat."

"Brains are actually organs," I say.

"What was that, Marcus?"

"Nothing."

We gently stretch first, then we run some laps around the basement until we're out of breath. Then, we do some sit-ups and push-ups and like a million jumping jacks. After that, we walk around the basement, shaking out our hands and arms and legs and feet. We end the session with more gentle stretching.

"And we're done!" Dad always says at the end of our workouts. Everyone claps.

That evening after crossword puzzle time, Ginny suggests we make shadow puppets. We hang a sheet up on the indoor drying line and use the big flashlight. Even Mom joins in and we retell the story of the Princess and the Pea.

I have to pee in the middle of the night and the big flashlight dies as soon as I turn it on. So I fumble around for the radio on the shelf near Mom and Dad, and I am thinking it is broken anyway, so why would we need to keep batteries in the radio if the radio isn't even working?

I feel around and find the radio. Then I feel around and find the battery pack at the back. And then it clicks open and my fingers scoop around in the empty space. No batteries here.

I don't want to miss the toilet or stub my toe in the dark, so I pee into the laundry sink instead. I worry Dad will wake up and hear me, but everyone stays fast asleep.

Radiation illness develops slowly. It cannot be spread to other people. Except for temporary nausea shortly after exposure, evidence of serious effects from radiation may only appear after a few days to three weeks. A combination of loss of hair, loss of appetite, increasing paleness, weakness, diarrhea, sore throat, bleeding gums and easy bruising indicate that the individual requires medical attention. Other symptoms such as nausea and vomiting may be caused by fright, worry, food poisoning, pregnancy and other common conditions and should not be taken as positive proof of radiation sickness.

There is no such thing as vanilla rainbow sprinkle birthday cake down here in Subterranea. Instead, I get a gelatinous cylinder of cranberry sauce with an emergency candle stuck in the middle.

Happy birthday to you!
Happy birthday to you!
Happy birthday, dear Marcus!
Happy birthday to you!
I make a wish and blow out the candle.
"What did you wish for, baby?" asks Mom.

"I wished for everything to go back to the way it was before," I say.

"Are you retarded?" says Ginny. "You're not supposed to say your wish out loud! That way, it'll never come true."

"Oh. I didn't know that."

Mom starts to cry.

"Listen, I got you a present," says Ginny, a little more softly. "It's a birthday balloon. Everyone should get to have balloons on their birthday." She hands me a blue surgical glove blown up and tied off at the wrist. We bounce it around the room like a beach ball.

Last year for my birthday, I had real balloons. Last year, I had real presents.

It was sunny and it was summer and we threw a barbecue and there was me and Ginny and Mom and Dad, plus my friends Craigger and Jake from school and their moms and dads. Ginny was allowed to bring her best friend, Carol. And a bunch of our neighbours were there, too. Including the Williams family who were Black and who had just moved across the street. When they showed up, Dad slapped his forehead and said really loudly that he'd forgotten to pick up the fried chicken and watermelon. A few people laughed, although I don't know why. Mr. Williams didn't laugh. But I don't think he's the kind of guy who smiles or laughs too much, anyway.

Us kids got to drink all the orange pop and cream soda we wanted – my two most favourite drinks! The adults got to drink a special fruit punch my mom made. The colour of the punch matched the colour of Mom's blouse, which had a kind of tie-up thing in the middle above her belly button. It looked really nice with her dark blue shorts that had little white anchors on them. Mom told us the punch was only for the grown-ups. I said I was the birthday boy and I should be able to eat and drink and do whatever I wanted, but she said that I would hate the taste.

"It's like Brussels sprouts," she said. "Kids don't like the same tastes grown-ups do." I thought she meant the fruit punch tasted like Brussels sprouts. I stuck with my cream soda.

Mom lost her balance a little and spilled some punch on Mr. Williams while she was refilling everyone's glasses after we ate. Dad got mad and called Mom a useless klutz in front of everyone. He also called her another word that sounded like *klutz*, but I didn't know what it meant.

"Relax, Jim," said Mr. Williams. "It was an accident."

"I'm so sorry," said Mom. "I'll get you cleaned up." And he followed her inside.

I went inside after them because I had to go pee but then I got distracted and started playing with my new The Thing action figure in my room. When I came out, I saw Mr. Williams in the laundry room without a shirt on. Mom must have spilled some punch on her red blouse, too, because Mr. Williams was helping her to untie it. I told them I was having a good birthday so far and when they were finished doing laundry, was it time for cake?

For wounds, you must 1) stop bleeding (haemorrhage) and 2) keep out germs (infection). Cover the wound with a clean dressing to keep out dirt and germs. Bandage it on firmly to stop the bleeding. If a wound is bleeding profusely, hold it firmly with your hand until you can secure an emergency dressing. Any thick pad of clean, soft, compressible material large enough to cover the wound will make a good dressing. Clean handkerchiefs, towels, sanitary pads, tissue handkerchiefs or sheets all make good emergency dressing.

On the bottom of Ginny's big toe, there's a blood blister that looks like a drop of squid ink behind her skin. It's sick. She lets me touch it as long as I don't push on it too hard.

"It's from doing all of those stupid calisthenics," Ginny whispers into my ear so Dad can't hear. Her shoes are pink with glitter but also see-through. They're called jellies. The jellies rub on Ginny's feet and make them hurt.

"We're a family," Dad yells. "Nobody whispers in a family. There are no secrets between flesh and blood."

"It's just my toe," says Ginny. "It hurts, okay?"

"Which toe?"

She shows him.

"Your mother will get that all bandaged up," says Dad. "Why are you wearing those horrible plastic nets on your feet, anyway?"

"They're my summer shoes, so they're what I'm wearing," Ginny says. "If you want, I can just quickly run upstairs and grab my sneakers."

"Very funny," says Dad. "It won't hurt you to sit with the discomfort for a while. Discomfort builds character."

"Fine," pouts Ginny. "Can I go to the washroom?"

"You've already gone twice today," Dad says. "Hold it in for a while."

Dad lectures us every day on the importance of minimizing our trips to the washroom. We have to conserve the toilet tissue we have, because it's not like Mom can just run to the corner store to get us some more.

"Well, I have to go again. Okay?"

"Just let her go, Jim," says Mom.

"Number one or number two?" he asks.

"Number two."

Dad carefully measures out four squares of toilet paper and hands them to Ginny. If she had said number one, she'd have only been given two squares. I know she's been saying number two when it's just a number one so she can get more toilet paper. We are already learning the tricks of Subterranea.

Ginny has been in the washroom for a long time. Girls usually take longer than boys, but I'm starting to wonder what the heck she's doing in there. I wish I'd been counting. I bet she's been in the crapper for at least a thousand seconds.

"Ginny!" says Dad. "Hop to it!"

"Ginny, honey?" says Mom. "Everything okay in there?"

"Mom?" Ginny cries out.

Mom runs over and opens the door to the washroom.

"What is it, hon?" says Mom.

"Close the door!" Ginny yells. "Close it! Close the door!"

The door shuts quickly behind them. I can hear them whispering.

"No whispering!" shouts Dad. "Enough whispering!"

"The madness of the Mole Man!" I announce. It's from *Fantastic Four.*

"Marcus, be quiet," says Dad.

Mom opens the bathroom door. "Marcus, honey," she says. "Be a doll and grab us the first aid kit, please?"

"Why?" asks Dad. "Is she hurt? What in the hell is going on in there?"

"Nothing much," says Mom. "She's fine. Just needs a little cleanup."

I'm looking through our supplies to try to find the first aid kit but things have been moved around. I find the package of emergency candles they used for my birthday cranberry sauce.

"This says 'Keep Out of Reach of Children,'" I say, holding them up to Dad. "I'm a child. These shouldn't be down so low."

"Don't be a smart aleck," says Dad.

"My name is Marcus," I say. "Not Alec."

"Goddamnit, get out of my sight before I smack you, you annoying little faggot!"

I retreat to a corner to count the floor tiles again and just go into my brain, go into my brain, go into my brain. Mom asks for the first aid kit again through the door and I hear her voice like a dream but I don't respond. I think Dad goes. He knocks and Mom takes the kit. I hear a tiny bit of what they say, even though it's mostly quiet. Even though it's mainly whispers.

"Just a minor scrape. It's nothing."

"You know I know it's something."

"Well, we just used a little gauze, that's all."

"What was the gauze for?"

"Jim," says Mom. "For God's sakes, you didn't think to stockpile any sanitary napkins?"

What happened next happened really fast. Or it happened in slow motion. It's hard to tell. I can't really describe it, but when I think about it now, it feels like a movie. It happened when I had counted only fifty-nine tiles.

Dad screaming. Ginny and Mom crying. Dad calling Ginny words that I'd never even heard before. Ginny calling Dad words that I'd only ever heard on the playground. The next thing I knew, Dad's giant hands were wrapped around Ginny's skinny chicken neck and he was screaming and Mom was screaming and I was screaming but Ginny couldn't scream because she couldn't breathe and then I couldn't breathe but my heart was pounding so fast, so fast and I was thinking about Mister Fantastic and wishing he could come and rescue us but then I remembered how he couldn't because he lived in comic books. I had to be Mister Fantastic. I had no choice.

"Annihilus!" I scream. "The living death that walks! *It's clobberin' time!*"

And so I attack Annihilus. I throw myself at his monstrous form and stab him in the back of the knee with my precision compass. All the way deep. The monster howls and falls to the ground, hitting his head on the hard, white tiles below. There is a sound like clattering metal. A silver key at the feet of the beast. I make a dive for it. Instinct.

"Let's go!" Ginny says in a strange gargly voice, gesturing toward the door.

"But the fallout!"

"It's better than being here. It's better than this."

Ginny takes the key from me and unlocks the door from the inside, slamming it behind us. I can still hear Mom weeping, Annihilus roaring.

Feet pounding the ground, blood singing in our brains, we dash through the house, open the front door and burst into the screaming white daylight.

*

"Here," says Mom, opening a can of orange pop and plunging a white straw into the dark opening. "Have a sip, okay? You haven't had anything to eat or drink this whole trip."

I'm staring out the smudged window at the lake. It's the biggest of the Great Lakes. It even has a big name. Lake Superior looks more like an ocean to me than a lake – the waves are huge and grey and seem to lap up all around us. The train gently rocks back and forth and I am terrified that if I get up and move around, shifting my weight from one side of the car to the other, we'll all fall into the dark, churning water.

"Not thirsty," I tell her. She makes a frustrated clicking sound and lowers the blue plastic tray in front of me. She puts my pop in the rounded hole moulded into the tray so it doesn't spill.

"Grandma hasn't seen you since Christmas. She'll be so surprised at how much taller you've grown." I keep staring out the window, my nose against the glass. Ginny has been asleep across the aisle from us for the whole trip. I can hear her snoring. If I tell her when she wakes up that she was snoring, she'll get mad. "I don't snore, idiot!" she'll say, and sock me in the ribs.

"How long are we going to be staying with Grandma?" I ask. "A week or ...?"

"We've been over this," Mom says quietly.

"Well, I'm just triple-checking – *okay?*"

In my backpack, I've stuffed in as many comic books as I could. *Spider-Man*, *Batman*, *He-Man*, *Richie Rich* and a couple of *Archie* digests – for Ginny, in case she forgot. I also packed a university math textbook, my protractor set, the miniature abacus Grandma got me for Christmas last year and some granola bars. Mom said there would be food on the train that we could buy, but you never know. You always have to be prepared. In case of an emergency, you know. Like a fire. Or nuclear fallout. Or forcible confinement. That last one was what I heard the policeman say when he was filing the report.

Mr. Williams was watering the front lawn when he saw Ginny and me making a break for it. Within a minute of explaining, he brought us into the house and dialled 911.

"Richard Williams, 38 Cherokee Lane," he said and then told us kids everything was going to be okay from here on in. Everything was going to be fine.

I look over at my mom on the train. Her shoulders are heaving along, even though the bumpiest part of the ride is past us now. Her cheeks are wet. I hold her hand. With the other hand, I take a sip of orange pop. It's cold and sweet and the fizz tickles my nose and make me hiccup.

It's raining outside and the waves on the lake are huge and greyer than the sky. They look dangerous. There was a tsunami last fall, in France. I saw the pictures on the news. Some people died. But no, these waves are not the bad kind. These waves are the okay kind. The go-away-without-hurting-anyone kind. They do look pretty big but I think that's just the wind. These waves, they're supposed to be here. They're just doing what they're supposed to be doing – washing away everything old and sick and broken and dying and bringing fresh clean newness along with it.

Underwater Calisthenics

AFTER THE THIRD PREGNANCY TEST I SHOPLIFTED from the drugstore, I asked Miranda what I should do about it. On a piece of stationery bordered by dancing teddy bears in pink tutus, she wrote out a list in her puffy script: "Natural Cures," double underlined in pink. The scented marker made my underwear drawer reek like bubble gum for days.

I followed Miranda's list like gospel. One hundred jumping jacks before breakfast. Loads of parsley. Mug after mug of strong black coffee. ("Since when do you like coffee?" asked Aunt Ruth. "Since always.") As the caffeine cartwheeled around my system, I'd swim violent lengths at the community centre. Hard, punishing strokes. An imperfect, floundering butterfly until I choked back water and felt like passing out. I threw up triumphantly once or twice afterwards, but later realized it was probably just morning sickness.

At church, the other girls asked God for clear skin and Friday night dates. I prayed for cramps and blood. And forgiveness for the sinful acts I'd committed that got me into this mess, offering an extra special sorry to Jesus Christ if He'd ever seen me and Trevor going at it.

The first time I attempted to fall down the stairs, I teetered for several minutes but didn't have the guts. I begged Miranda to push me on my second try. She didn't throw enough power behind the shove so I just kind of got turned around, landing a few steps below her. We laughed in disbelief at my carpet-burnt knees until the tears came. I didn't try again after that.

"If I have an abortion," I said as Miranda dabbed Polysporin on my knees, "will I be sending the doctor to hell for murder?"

"It's their *job*," Miranda said, rolling her eyes. I noticed she hadn't answered my question.

Aunt Ruth had been raising me since I was little. She was religious and sent me to Sunday school to make sure I "grew up straight" unlike "that mother of yours." (My mother ran off with a truck driver who was not my father when I was five.) I learned in Sunday school that dead unbaptized babies go to this place called limbo. Limbo is not quite bad and not quite good. I picture a huge white room with endless rows of chubby babies just floating around, shaking silver rattles and cooing at each other. It doesn't sound too terrible, actually.

Once, a mouse got into our Sunday school classroom. It ran all over like a little windup toy. Miss Alma jumped onto a chair and screamed, "Somebody kill it!" All the kids tried stomping on the mouse as it scurried by. Eventually, Miranda's older brother, Michael, trapped it under a wastepaper basket. Everyone clapped. But we could still hear it fluttering and scratching in its tin prison. The janitor came and crushed its tiny body under the weight of the Old Testament. Miss Alma, quiet for once in her life, herded us into the antechamber to wait for our families. I asked Miss Alma if the janitor was going to hell for killing one of God's bright and beautiful creatures. She pretended to not hear me.

"As you may know, abortion is legal now," sighed the nurse at the clinic, pushing pamphlets into my hands. "But adoption is an option worth considering."

I parroted this sentence at Miranda and she laughed.

"Like anyone's going to want to adopt your retarded baby!"

"My baby's not retarded," I said, with only a little bit of hesitation.

"Obviously it's going to be retarded," said Miranda. "It's got a full retard for a dad."

Miranda had introduced me to Trevor on Canada Day. He was Michael's friend. Trevor and Michael also went to the same school. ("A special school," Miranda called it, lolling her tongue around and slapping at her chest.) It sounded just like our school except the kids took fewer classes and called the teachers by their first names. Trevor and Michael were pretty much best friends and hung out everywhere and all the time, like me and Miranda. Trevor is all kinds of tall and skinny and Michael is short and kind of fat. Miranda called them Bert and Ernie to be mean. Miranda said they were probably gay for each other.

The thing about Miranda's brother, Michael, is that his spine is crooked. He wears a brace but you can't really tell because he mostly wears loose-fitting sports jerseys. He also wears winter toques all the time, even in summer. Michael almost died when he was a baby. He had water on the brain and doctors had to drill in a tap-like-thing to keep his head from expanding like a hot air balloon. I pictured it being like my bathroom sink tap, with a side for cold water and one for hot. Now the tap or whatever is on the inside. It's called a shunt.

"Why did your head have so much water in it?" I'd asked him once when we were younger.

"We are all a large percentage of water," he replied, before showing me his baseball card collection. Since we didn't have a Major League Baseball team, he rooted for Toronto. Kelly Gruber and Mookie Wilson were his favourite Blue Jays. He knew all of their statistics off by heart. Height, weight, RBIS. I thought baseball was boring but I didn't say anything. Michael had an odd way of speaking and got picked on a lot, but he was always nice to me so I made sure I was always nice back.

Michael brought Trevor along to a Canada Day barbecue at the park. Trevor was actually really cute, which I hadn't expected from the person Miranda insisted on calling Bert. He had these crazy blue eyes and so many freckles that they all kind of blended into each other.

"Hey there, Bert," Miranda pushed two fingers into the concave of Trevor's chest. "This is my friend Bethany."

"Hi," I said. "I brought butter tarts."

"So I guess I'd better try one to make sure they're not poisonous." Trevor smiled at me and took a bite out of the one I was holding, so I was feeding him. Miranda shot me a disgusted look.

"You'll have to make some just for me sometime," he said, snaking a skinny arm around the small of my back.

"Ugh, she just got them from Mariposa Market," said Miranda. "They're famous, you know. You can buy them basically whenever you want."

Miranda looked me up and down. Then she turned her back and made a big show about announcing it was time to light the sparklers.

Trevor asked me for my number and called me the next day. We started hanging out a lot. I started seeing less and less of Miranda. Whenever I did see her, she made a point of telling me what a true loser I was dating and what did I even see in him, anyway?

My period was really late and I'd had two positive pregnancy tests when Trevor drove just the two of us to Bass Lake. We stopped at a gas station along the way and got freezies that made our lips turn blue and a can of Mountain Dew to share. Right after he parked, we started making out in the car but then I had to open the window to puke blue sugar water into the bushes.

"You sick or something?"

I figured that was as obvious an opening as any.

He got out of the car and sat on the side of the hill. I followed and sat down beside him. Trevor snapped a long blade of grass that had gone to seed and chewed on it, looking like a farmer chomping on some straw and inspecting his fertile acres.

"So what makes you think it's even mine?"

It felt like a slap. I wanted to slap back.

"You think I go around doing it with every boy in Orillia?"

Trevor hugged his pale grasshopper legs to his chest. I started counting the freckles on his face because I didn't know what else to do. I made it up to twenty.

"So what are you going to do about it?"

I shrugged.

He stood up. "So maybe you should tell me when you know."

He sucked back the dregs of the pop, tossed the can onto the grass and headed back toward the car. I didn't feel like following him.

After that, I figured we were broken up.

Last summer, I leapt into lake water so cold I could barely take in air when I surfaced. I felt that same breathlessness when one of our wooden kitchen chairs, wielded by my aunt Ruth, made full contact with my abdomen. She had found one of the pregnancy tests in the trash.

When I managed to wedge in a breath, I bolted. Aunt Ruth chased after me for a moment, screaming that I was a Jezebel and a whore, that I was going to burn in hell for eternity and that I owed her a new chair.

I sprinted and sobbed for ten blocks before leaning on Miranda's doorbell. It was Michael who answered.

"Greetings, Bethany," he said. "Would you like to come in for a cup of water?"

When Miranda's mom came home, I told her what happened through tears. Lainie, which is what I'd always called her, held me in her ample arms and sighed. "Poor sweet soul. I'll drive you to a clinic in Toronto in a heartbeat. You just let me know, angel."

Miranda raised an eyebrow when she saw me sipping chamomile tea on the couch.

"Bethany is having a rough go at home, dear heart," said Lainie. "She'll be staying with us for a while. She'll sleep in your room."

"But I don't want to share my bed."

"Sleep on the chesterfield, then!" Lainie slammed a fist on the coffee table. "Christ, girl! Where's your head?"

Miranda's bedspread smelled like Love's Baby Soft and stale towels. The wall facing me was a constellation of glow-in-the-dark star stickers that I picked at idly while waiting for sleep. I usually slept on my stomach, but the mottled bruises splayed across my belly kept me from that. Miranda talked in her sleep. She'd otherwise stopped speaking to me entirely.

I was alone a lot. Miranda worked at a day camp and Lainie was back and forth at odd hours, taking on as many cleaning shifts as she could handle. She used to cook and clean at one private home exclusively, but stopped after the client got too "familiar."

"Just because they're paying you for one job, they think they're entitled to another," she said, shaking her head. "Never let yourself be alone with men, Bethany, no good can come of it." She regarded my still-flat belly with pity. "But you already knew that."

Michael went to summer school almost every day and had gone as stone silent as his sister. I wondered if he felt weird about what had happened between Trevor and me. Or worse, if he hated me because of it. Maybe Trevor said awful things about me. Maybe he called me a lying whore. Maybe Michael believed him.

One day in late August, instead of immediately hiding in his room, Michael disappeared into the kitchen. He emerged a few minutes later, presenting a plate of perfect grilled cheese sandwiches. We ate them while watching *The Price Is Right*.

"Have you ever noticed how no one seems to bid on the first Showcase Showdown?" said Michael. "They just pass and wait for the next one."

"The next one's always better," I replied.

"Not always," he said.

We watched in silence for a minute. The second lady won the first showcase. The host reminded us to have our pets spayed or neutered.

"I want to see your scar," I said. Michael hesitated for a moment before doffing his toque and tilting his head toward me, smacking the fleshy pink horseshoe on top.

"Do you think it'll bring me luck if I touch it?" I asked him.

"It hasn't brought me much luck, so I don't know why you'd bother."

I touched it anyway.

*

Underwater calisthenics replaced the frantic butterfly as my pool ritual. Subaquatic jumping jacks, handstands and back floats. The floats were my favourite because they blocked out the world. I'd dip my head back just enough to have the water cover my ears. The echo chamber of the pool deck was muted, the world made gelatinous. I'd stretch out my arms and legs like a snow angel, the water supporting me like a million tiny hands.

I watched a Mommies and Toddlers class starting in the shallow end and became very aware of the tiny swimming pool inside me. Somewhere in there, a veined jelly bean floated and throbbed. What do embryos even dream about? They only know the womb, so they must only dream about heartbeats. And liquid. And floating. I positioned my body into another back float.

"We are all a large percentage of water," I said. The fluid amplified the sound of my own voice, words humming within a skull that felt as vast and as white as limbo. "Adoption is an option worth considering." Salty tears and chlorinated water stung my eyes in equal measure.

As an experiment, I curled up into the fetal position and promptly sank.

In Heaven, Everything Is Fine

THE HOUSE ON DURANT AVENUE WAS ONE OF THOSE generic postwar brick bungalows, but to me, it was home. It had cheerful flower boxes in the windows that my mother had painted herself and smooth concrete steps leading to the forest green front door. On my computer screen, the house looked the same as it did in my memory, if somewhat pixelated. And just as they often do in my memory, my dead mom and dead dad sat on the porch, holding hands.

Five hundred miles away from the street I grew up on, I was getting my MFA in Creative Writing in Amherst. I hadn't seen the house in months; not since the winter they both passed.

Mom slipped on the ice on the front steps, even though Dad made sure they were as heavily salted as every meal she had ever made for us. Surgery went well; she had been expected to make a full recovery. Instead, her body began to shut down, quadrant by quadrant, like a starship on reserve power. Minor setbacks became serious new threats. Every day, there was a new complication, some treacherous new obstacle to overcome.

I'd shuttled back and forth between Boston and Toronto, sleeping primarily on Greyhound buses and in hard-backed chairs at Sunnybrook Hospital. My studies suffered, but I had to be there for my mom and dad. While Mom slept, I laid my head on Dad's lap like I used to do when I was a child and he'd speak soothingly of the doctor's genuine optimism. I always loved my father's voice. It was gentle and calm and I believed every word he'd ever said. He promised me that life would get back to normal soon and Mom would be back to cooking too-salty meat and potatoes, singing funny little made-up songs to herself and nagging us both in no time flat. A few days after Christmas, it became clear that the accumulation of complications was insurmountable. Ten days before their wedding anniversary, Mom's body failed her and all of us.

Early in the new year, Dad suffered a massive heart attack at the men's club while playing cards. His friends told me he had held the winning hand. A straight flush of hearts ending on the king and queen.

I dealt with the funerals and the house in a sort of fog and booted it back to the States as soon as I could. To distract myself from fresh grief and the disorientation of not being able to call or visit my parents anymore, I threw myself headlong into my novel, working gruelling hours and living on protein bars and black coffee. Sleep became the enemy. Somewhere along the way, I acquired a near-crippling anxiety disorder. I rarely left my room, let alone the house. I broke into cold sweats and was racked by violent panic attacks that left me trembling. I kept a paper bag next to my computer, heaving air into it as required.

I couldn't remember the last time I had had a solid bowel movement. It hadn't occurred to me to masturbate in weeks.

"We need to talk," said my girlfriend, who told me she didn't want to be that asshole who breaks up with someone roiling in fresh grief, but who ended up being that asshole anyway. The blessing of it was that the end of my relationship was layered upon so much existing, throbbing, radiating pain that I barely felt it at all. It was like getting a paper cut after breaking all of your limbs.

Not unlike writing, grieving is a messy, illogical process. It comes in spurts and manifests itself in many different forms. Grief and chronic anxiety are twin shape-shifting beasts that will pin you to the mat, but never when you're looking directly at them.

I shouldn't have been surprised by how mentally and physically incapacitated I would be in the year that followed. Like most overly sensitive neurotics, I'd been quietly preparing myself for the deaths of my parents practically since birth. They had been older, having already given up on ever having children when I surprised them in mid-life. I was well cared for, but despite this, our relationship had always been strained. I was embarrassed by them as a kid and a teenager – these unfashionable white-haired people who were often mistaken for my grandparents. In the cooler months, Mom wore fur coats with matching fur hats, which was humiliating during my vegan anarchist days. Dad wore thermal underwear, went to church and sometimes smoked a pipe. I never came out to them. More than my own happiness, I understood from their nagging and their encouragements laced with longing that they had wanted my life's trajectory to mimic their own. It had not and never would. I was an artist and a weirdo and a deeply closeted queer person who didn't want a traditional job and never wanted kids. Had they known the whole story of who I was, I felt like I would have been a colossal disappointment to them. And here is the worst part: I had loved them dearly and missed them monumentally, but their twin departures had been something of a strange relief. Every bone in my body had sighed, every muscle relaxed. I was finally free to be myself. The guilt I felt about this was enormous.

Acute grief hit like a tsunami in July on what would have been my father's eightieth birthday. Shades drawn, I sobbed in the semi-darkness of my bedroom all day, stopping only when my worried roommate gently rapped on my door to quietly ask if I'd like some tomato soup.

I was bleary-eyed and exhausted when I typed my childhood address into a search engine, pulling up a digitized map of our street. I needed to see the house again – our house. I clicked the RealView tab, revealing digital photos snapped by a behemoth tech company already halfway to running the world. Durant Avenue was alive in lush summer hues. I scrolled a little until I got a clear view of our house, then zoomed all the way in.

That's when I saw my dead parents on our porch. Mom was seated on the right. She was wearing her favourite blue housedress with the little white fabric rosette buttons. Dad was on the left, wearing an undershirt and a sun hat. Their hands were latched together. They looked relaxed and happy. My throat tightened around a hot marble of grief. RealView had preserved my parents in digital amber. Someday soon these photos would be updated, overwritten. My mother and father would disappear from our porch forever. I fell into fresh sobs, but was strangely comforted by these sweetly familiar figures. Although they were looking out onto Durant Avenue, I felt as though they were looking right at me. I could almost hear their voices. For the first time since their funerals, I slept the whole night through.

I didn't revisit my electric parents until there was frost on my windowpanes. The holidays were fast approaching. I would spend them in Massachusetts, alone. My parents were dead. The house had been sold. I'd lost touch with even my closest friends in the past year. There was no good reason to return to Toronto.

"Merry Christmas, Mom and Dad," I said to the images on my computer screen. Mom was wearing a pink housedress, her silver hair in curlers. Dad was wearing his ratty old brown robe, a red mug of coffee in hand. I squinted hard. Hadn't my mother been wearing her blue dress earlier? Surely they couldn't be wearing different things than when I first saw them here? Unless it was an updated photo, but that made no sense at all. My memory must have been playing tricks on me. I chalked my confusion up to my past emotional state. I had cried so long and hard that day, it was a wonder I could even see the screen at all.

I dreamt of them both that night. They were decorating a huge and beautiful Christmas tree with popcorn garlands, silver tinsel and skulls encrusted with jewels.

"Come," said Dad in his soothing voice. "You're the tall one in the family. We're going to need you to put the star on the tree." The star was made out of black glass and warped my reflection into old age. I tried to reach the top of the tree but watched as my strong, young arm withered into that of an old crone. I screamed as my arm fell to dust. The glass star floated in mid-air for a long moment before shattering. That's when I woke up.

Winter dissolved into spring. The first draft of my manuscript was more than halfway complete. I came up for air and decided to spend the day being good to myself. I went for a long walk, finding snowdrops and crocuses along the way. I got a haircut. I went for beers with some people in my program. It had been months since I'd felt so relaxed, so at peace. When I got home, my head pleasantly twirling with music and alcohol and interesting conversation, it occurred to me that I should take a screen capture of my parents' old place and their porch idling for the sake of posterity. The RealView car might do its rounds this summer and pave over them with a new, updated photograph of Durant Avenue. Same porch, new family.

I pulled up the address and there they sat. They were both wearing black, as if having just returned from a funeral. Mom's eyes were half-hidden by a sheer dark veil I had never seen before. Both of her hands covered her mouth. Dad was in his good black suit – the one I'd buried him in – and seemed to be holding something white in one hand. I zoomed in closer to see five playing cards – a straight flush, ending on the king and queen of hearts.

I yanked the computer's power cord from the wall and promptly called my psychiatrist.

Months later, the final draft of my manuscript was complete. It was an updated version of the Greek myth of Persephone. The one with the pomegranate seeds and the abduction and seasonal rape in perpetuity. The ancient Greeks loved stories about rape. Especially as perpetrated by the gods, because they were righteous and untouchable – not unlike today's athletes and politicians. My take on the myth was this: A glamorous Hollywood actress is blackmailed into marrying a mob boss twice her age to settle her manager-lover's massive gambling debts. There were mountains of cocaine! Loads of orgies! A subtle commentary on the toxicity of unchecked wealth and power in men in the 1980s and beyond. I intended to shop it to agents and publishers under a slick male pseudonym, practically guaranteeing its publication. Maybe even some prestigious literary awards. I'd rub elbows with famous white male authors at parties before talking shit about them behind their backs.

As I emerged from my writing haze, I was feeling more mentally stable. I was sleeping a solid six hours a night. Eating again of my own volition. It had been weeks since my last panic attack. I thought of my parents. Of how proud they would have been of the completion of my novel. With the help of my psychiatrist, I had understood that what I saw on RealView last time – the veil, the cards – was some nightmarish figment of my frail psyche in the depths of grief, mounting stress, lack of sleep and dark, endless days. I was clear-headed now. Almost back to normal. My psychiatrist suggested that, during this time of relative mental and emotional stability, it might be a good time to visit my parents again via RealView to say goodbye. There was something deeply comforting about the fact that they were there, waiting for me inside my computer screen whenever I felt like visiting them. But I had to let them go.

I cautiously pulled up our street number and looked at the occupants of the house on Durant Avenue. Blue floral dress. Jaunty sun hat. Just as I'd remembered them. Just as I'd seen them the first time. Just as they existed in my mind and my memory. I exhaled in relief.

Then: movement.

I double blinked. Squinted. Cocked my head. A computer glitch? Light reflected by a dust mote?

No.

My mother's mouth was *moving*. Actually moving. Open and shut. Like a ventriloquist dummy or a hungry baby bird, soundless but insistent.

I rubbed my eyes and she stopped moving. I exhaled in a gust. It was then that my father's mouth began to move. His little pixelated hand turned and shifted, pointing in my direction. With a slight flick of his wrist, my father indicated the bottom right corner of my computer screen. He was pointing toward the headphone jack.

I barely recognized my own voice when I spoke.

"Oh ... God ... you're asking me to plug the headphones in?" The tiny parents in my computer nodded their tiny heads.

I plugged my headphones into the jack with shaking hands. The first sound I heard was something like a wind tunnel. Whooshes and white noise, airy and vast. I could then make out my mother's voice, sounding groggy, as though she had just woken up from a long nap. Which, I suppose, she had.

"Yoooooou," said my mother, her moaning muted and hoarse. Not quite her voice, yet.

The unmistakable sound of my father's voice, then. His was louder and stronger. It sliced through my rib cage and into my heart. I remembered replaying the last voice message I ever got from him, listening to his soothing tones over and over and over again. I was grief-stricken and enraged when my telecom provider unceremoniously deleted it from my voice mail inbox. I called their customer service line in tears and accused them of stealing his voice from me.

"Just calling to see that you made your bus on time," he had said. "Talk to you later, sweetheart. Buh-bye now." It had been, I'd thought, the very last time I would hear my father's voice. And yet, here it was again. That voice that I had loved my entire life. That voice that I had struggled to remember perfectly after his death. The more time passed, the less I could hear him in my head. Time and memory warp everything. Forgetting the exact sound of the voice of a person you love is the cruellest kind of forgetting.

"Whyyyy," Dad said, his finger pointing outward, as though accusing me of something.

My parents were dead. Definitively and thoroughly. I had ordered the flowers and the caskets myself, sat numbly through their services, written the obituaries, sold their house, mourned their loss with every breath of the past eighteen months. And yet, here they were in RealView's two dimensions, desperately trying to communicate with me. It must be about something important. A warning? Were they attempting to save me from some horrific unknown fate? This was miraculous. This was terrifying. I felt privileged to bear witness to it. I listened closely.

"Whyyyy," said Dad. "Whyyyyyyyy don't you have a boyfriend yet? Don't you want to start a family before it's too late?"

"Yooooouuu," said Mom. "Yooooooou should stop it with the writing and clean that sty of yours. Did we raise you in a barn?"

In death as in life. It was oddly comforting.

My happiness was all that mattered now. I kissed the computer screen twice, closed the tab and emerged from my room, eager to rejoin the real, living, breathing, pulsating, unnerving world at last.

Five Full-Colour Dreams of a Young Marie Curie

Dream #1:
Diogenes Lights the Lamp

"Come, child." Diogenes takes me by the hand. "Let me show you the way." His fingers are gnarled and twisted, ancient twigs. A delicate accordion of tendons glide under papyrus skin, thin and translucent. I feel every knob and sharpness, the very bone of him. A feral dog at his feet barks a warning.

"You are a seeker of knowledge," he tells me. "You are a seeker of truth."

The streets are deserted, although it is midday. He stands still for a moment to light his lamp, though we are already drenched in sunlight.

"You would be surprised by the difference a single light can make."

We arrive at the temple. The oracle stands before us. She is wrapped in purple robes and crowned by floral garlands but her face is in shadows.

She crushes sweet herbs with a mortar and pestle, examines the slick entrails of a cat.

"Yours will be the sweet death of old age," she proclaims.

"Why does the oracle tell such lies?" The old man holds his lamp aloft, tremors racking his body.

Silence fills our ears as we leave the temple.

The sun slides down into a crimson and violet bed.

We curl up together in his red clay urn, a hard and unforgiving womb for sleeping. The night is cold and his lamp has long been extinguished.

Dream #2: Babcia's Hearth

I sit quietly on my babcia's lap, plaiting her long silver hair. I am six years old. We share a name.

A blue and orange fire burns brightly and steadily in the hearth of the tower room. Steam rises from the cooking pot, like ghostly souls of the righteous floating upwards after the Divine Judgment.

"Come, Manya," Babcia says. Her voice is dark honey flowing over gravel. "The water is ready for us now."

Rows of pierogi are laid out like fleshy thumbs on my grandmother's table. We examine them closely, pinching the edges of the few errant ones tighter still.

"Remember, babisiu –" Babcia takes my chin between thumb and forefinger, looking serious "– education is the most important thing. Being a wife. Becoming a mother. There is time for that. You must put your studies above all things. Do you understand?"

"Yes, Babcia."

As we gingerly drop the soft, pale pierogi into the cooking pot, I look hard at the fire. The source of the strong, unwavering flame is a Bunsen burner.

Dream #3: Serpentilia

I am lying prone in a white tub in a bone-white room. The air is rich and warm with the fragrance of lavender, but the tub is full of ice.

A jade-skinned serpent slithers through a tiny window just out of reach. He joins me in the tub, wrapping himself around one of my legs and then the other, crimson tongue darting. Though unable to move, I am unafraid.

He looks at me with vermilion eyes. He does not speak but we understand one another.

At night, the serpent sleeps coiled on my belly. I am comforted by the weight of him. I sing Polish lullabies as we drift off.

Lulaj, lulaj moje dziecie
pojedziamy do kościo.
Lulaj, lulaj do ziecora
aż ci matka przyjdzie z pol.
Lulaj, lulaj stari hulaj,
a hulajka psiekła jȧjka.
Usiadła sie na zapsiecku
psiekła jȧjka w tygielec.

I am feeding the serpent boiled eggs for breakfast when he lashes out, fangs sinking into my wrist. My hand and forearm swell up like a Zeppelin. I do what I can to tend to the wound, but it festers and before long, it turns dark as ash.

I am lying prone in a spirophore in a bone-white room. The air is cold and smells of bleach and death. All I can hear is my own deeply laboured breathing.

The serpent is nowhere to be seen.

I cannot be angry with him. Why should I be? All he has done is been true to his nature.

Dream #4: How Difficult Is a Woman's Life!

My mother coughs while cobbling in the corner. She is covered in blankets.

Lined up on the floor next to her are four identical pairs of leather shoes she has made for my brother and sisters. White and gleaming.

"Yours are almost ready," she says. She wipes her brow and I notice two parallel scars running down her right cheek. Mother shakes off the blankets to reveal a barefoot child latched to each breast. It is my brother, Jozef, and my sister Helena. Both are older than I. She cradles her children in the crooks of her arms. In her right hand, she holds a knife.

She begins to cough violently, her body spasming. The children squirm off her lap.

"Brew me some tea, Manya," she says weakly. I do what I'm told. I bring my mother hot tea in a special china cup, hoping to cheer her. It is a beautiful, delicate vessel painted with Bourbon lilies and a portrait of Louis Philippe of France.

Mother thanks me for the tea, which I hold to her lips. When she is finished, my hands slip and the teacup crashes to the floor, bursting into tiny pieces. I start to cry out of remorse and a fear of repercussion, but mother soothes me.

"Not to worry, my darling girl," she says. "Everything breaks."

In her small, almost translucent palms, she presents a perfect pair of red shoes.

"For your cousin's wedding," she says proudly. "And for you to wear to church where you may pray for the return of my health."

White shoes for my brother. White shoes for my sisters. Bright red shoes for me.

I caress the beautiful gift my mother has made me. My fingers come away wet with blood.

Dream #5: Red Right Hand

Saint Casimir is cheating at cards again.

"I used to be a prince, you know," he says, tucking the king of hearts into one velveteen sleeve. "And a very fine mathematician, besides!"

We are sitting in my tiny room in Paris. For my guest, I have laid out bread and water, sweet gherkins and tea.

"Bring me meat," he commands.

"But I have none."

"Bring me some chlodnik, then."

"This is all I have."

"Give me a moment," he says. "I shall conjure us a fine meal." He whirls his three hands in the air. Saint Casimir has one left hand and two right hands, which makes him particularly skilful at cheating. His rich velvet robes smell of woodsmoke and tuberose.

"You're a saint, not a conjuror," I tell him. "And anyway, saints aren't supposed to cheat."

"I'm not really a saint," Saint Casimir says. "I'm your cousin. We were once in love. You wanted to marry me. Do you remember?"

I remember, Casimir. How could I ever forget?

Saint Casimir plants the king and queen of hearts on the table, skewering them together with a dagger.

"I win," he says. "Would you like to play again?"

I tell him no. I tell him never again.

We eat the bread dipped in water because it is all I have.

Epilogue

My dreams have been so vivid lately that I can scarcely tell if I am sleeping or waking.

Riding an underwater train through cities and towns carved out of coral and glittering with sea glass. Lazing in hazy fields with my sisters, wildflower halos. Drinking bowls of poppies poured over with thick, sweet condensed milk.

A dear old friend swept me up in his arms. He laughed as he kissed my legs and feet. The sun was shining. I felt like a child.

I sometimes dream in colour, did you know that?

Are you awake, my love?

Radium Girl

ON HER WEDDING DAY, IMOGEN GLOWED.

We had given her the idea just a few days before. She didn't need much in the way of convincing.

"Oh! Wouldn't it be funny, though?"

"Togged to the bricks and then some, Moggy!"

We descended upon the bride's house on Clinton Street early that morning, a small giggling army brandishing paintbrushes and adhesive and Undark. Olive got to work on Imogen's pale hands, painting delicate bangles around her slender wrists after finishing her nails. I was in charge of her feet, gently massaging her heels with DuBarry special skin cream like she was the Queen of Sheba before painting her toenails with the radioluminescent paint. I asked our blushing girl if she wanted me to paint bangles on her ankles as well, but Olive shushed me.

"We don't want her looking cheap for her new husband, Elda," she said.

The jewellery came next. Carmela had the steadiest hand of all of us, so she was tasked with painting each delicate pearl of the green glowing necklace. It was amazing to watch Carmela work. She was as precise as a machine. Twirl, tongue, dab. Twirl, tongue, dab. She even painted Imogen's teeth afterwards so they'd glow in the dark.

"Charlie will never forget his wedding night," Carmela said and we all laughed. Who needs a boring old toothpaste smile when you can have Undark?

Shine, little glow-worm, glimmer, glimmer
Shine, little glow-worm, glimmer, glimmer!
Lead us lest too far we wander.
Love's sweet voice is calling yonder!

We sprinkled loose paint powder over the bride's freshly set pincurls like a blessing. Then, we turned out the lights and pulled the curtains tight to get the full effect.

Imogen looked like a fairy queen. She looked like an angel.

Shine, little glow-worm, glimmer, glimmer
Shine, little glow-worm, glimmer, glimmer
Light the path below, above,
And lead us on to love.

The stars in the sky paled in comparison to our girl and the hours fell away like brittle October leaves.

"I got blisters on my blisters!"

"Let's dance 'til our feet bleed!"

"Let's dance 'til our bones turn to dust!"

It had been a wonderful night.

The bride was simply luminous. Everyone said so.

*

Manufacturers have been quick to recognize the value of Undark. They apply it to the dials of watches and clocks, to electric push buttons, to the buckles of bed room slippers, to house numbers, flashlights, compasses, gasoline gauges, autometers and many other articles which you frequently wish to see in the dark.

We're the dial painter girls. Everyone knows us. Frankly, we're hard to miss.

They call us the ghost girls. After the sun sets, we light the way. Walking home, taking the train, always in pairs or packs. We glow like fireflies, the dust from the radium paint luminescent on our white collared smocks after a full day's work of painting watch dials. Sometimes we sneak up on our husbands and our beaus and our mothers and our fathers and say, "Boo!" We laugh in their faces before offering sweet apologetic kisses. Then we wash up and chop vegetables for supper.

The next time you fumble for a lighting switch, bark your shins on furniture, wonder vainly what time it is because of the dark – *remember Undark.* It shines in the dark.

It shines in the dark and so do we. Whenever I slip into bed next to my sister in our quiet, darkened room, my fingertips and lips glow green. No matter how much I wash or scrub, it's always there. It's just like in the summertime when we were children and used to eat mulberries by the dozen straight from the bush. It stained our mouths and fingers a dark purple and if it got on our clothes, our mothers got sore at us. It's a lot like that – only the radium paint doesn't wash off quite so easily.

Does Undark really contain radium? Most assuredly. It is radium, combined in exactly the proper manner with zinc sulphide, which gives Undark its ability to shine continuously *in the dark.*

161

I've had to stop hanging my work smock on the back of our bedroom door. I've been tucking it into a dresser ever since Allegra complained that the unwavering glow keeps her up at night.

It's a kind of magic, if you really think about it. A kind of sorcery.

And it's all ours.

*

The application of Undark is simple. It is furnished as a powder, which is mixed with an adhesive. The paste thus formed is painted on with a brush. It adheres firmly to any surface.

Imogen has a toothache. She's had it for days now, but today she's been complaining about it something awful.

"Call a dentist already." You can tell from Olive's voice that she has absolutely had it.

"Why don't you head on home, Moggy?" I ask her more gently.

Imogen goes all quiet. I know why. The wedding had cost her family a small fortune so she doesn't want to miss out on even a half-day's work. It's piecework we do here – we get paid by the dial. No dials, no moolah! Moggy's one of the fastest workers here, so an afternoon off would mean her missing out on a lot of dough. Right now, she needs every last red cent.

There's another reason why Imogen wants to be here today. She wants to meet him. We all want to meet him.

The Young Doctor is coming to visit the factory this afternoon. He's the inventor of the Undark paint we use to paint the watch dials. He's coming to Ottawa all the way from New Jersey. I've never met him before but I'm so grateful to him. He's the reason I have this job. And what a wonderful, high-paying, rip-roaringly fun job it is! Imagine we were all just regular old factory workers on an assembly line? Imagine we weren't seated together at these little wooden school desks at the former high school, the sunshine pouring in, gossiping the day away? Work feels like a kind of never-ending art class. Only our assignment is always the same: lip pointing the brushes so the tips are sharp and carefully painting the numbers and dials of watches with the Young Doctor's special paint so they'll glow in the dark.

"I hear the Young Doctor is handsome," whispers Carmela.

"I hear the Young Doctor is single," says Mary Catherine, smoothing her hair.

"Wear your best lipstick, Elda," Olive teases a little too loudly. I roll my eyes at her. I'm a single girl yet and Olive never lets me forget it.

At 12:15 p.m., the Young Doctor arrives. He is brought into the classroom by the plant manager, Mr. Weevil, and Miss Harrison, our supervisor. We are all still having lunch at our desks. We always eat lunch at our desks. Sometimes we go outside if it's nice out. But it hasn't been nice outside for a while.

"And here we have our dial painting studio," says Miss Harrison.

I am seated in the front row so I can get a real close look at him. It's true, what they say – he is very handsome. Not so young, though. Perhaps a man of forty. But I suppose that's young for an inventor. Whenever I think of inventors, I picture old white-haired men with large, bushy beards. Someone like Mr. Alexander Graham Bell, God rest his soul. I wouldn't have pegged a dark-eyed man with hollow cheeks, slicked-back hair, wearing a fine woollen coat for an inventor. He looks more like a poet. But I suppose Undark is a kind of poetry, in its own special way.

The Young Doctor gives the room a cursory glance before continuing his quiet conversation with Mr. Weevil. We pretend to be immersed in our lunches. For the first time I can ever remember, the classroom is almost completely silent.

"Doctor, I'd love for you to meet Elda here," says Miss Harrison. "She's one of our fastest dial painters."

"Pleased to meet ya, sir," I say. The Young Doctor says nothing.

"Why don't you watch Elda work for a spell?" says Miss Harrison. "You'll be amazed by her speed and artistry."

"Thank you, Miss Harrison," I say. Olive emphatically clears her throat. She'll be calling me teacher's pet later, no doubt about that.

I get out my paints and my brush. Miss Harrison brings me a new tray of dials to work on.

I bring my paintbrush to a sharp point with my lips, just as we have been taught to do before dipping it into Undark.

How thrilling! To be using an invention in the presence of the inventor!

"Don't do that!" snaps the Young Doctor.

"Do what?"

"Don't put the solution in your mouth," he hisses. "You'll get sick."

I look to Miss Harrison. She appears flummoxed but says nothing.

"Sir, I . . ."

From behind me, a loud sneeze from one of the girls. A clatter. Absolute silence. Until –

"My toof!" cries a voice.

Bedlam! Uproar! Laughter and shrieks and gasps and chatter and clatter from the classroom of dial painters.

Yet again, above the din: "My *toof*!"

I recognize the voice this time. It belongs to Imogen.

I whirl around to see her covering her mouth with her hands, her usually pale face red as a tomato with humiliation.

I turn back to the front of the classroom and my eyes search the checkerboard tiles of the classroom floor. There – in the corner just below the dusty chalkboard with a single Bible verse written on it in lacy script (Matthew 5:16 – *Let your light shine before men in such a way that they may see your good works, and glorify your Father who is in heaven.*) – lies a single yellowed tooth.

Just as suddenly as he had arrived, the Young Doctor is gone. He's quickly escorted to another room by Mr. Weevil. Miss Harrison flails her arms and attempts to get the room in order.

"Settle down, girls!" she yells. "That's quite enough! Stop that!"

But we are already too far gone.

*

Imogen rotates her wedding band around her ring finger.

"It's so loose these days," she says. Imogen has gone from a fleshy Irish Venus to a withered spindle. The gold barely touches her pallid skin now.

Carmela and I are visiting her in the hospital after work. Imogen herself hasn't been to work in weeks. Not since before Christmas. That's when things went really bad for her.

"It's anemia, mostly," she says, speaking more slowly than I've ever heard her speak. "Although that doesn't explain the jaw. They're still running some tests, I don't know."

Charlie had her admitted late last week. She'd been bleeding from her mouth and losing teeth for months, but suddenly she was weak as a kitten and nearly delirious from the pain in her jaw. The only thing that keeps her quiet and somewhat at peace with the world is a special kind of pain medicine fed directly into her body through the veins in her arms.

Imogen falls asleep during our visit. Her husband explains that she isn't able to stay awake for too many hours at a time these days.

"We'll get our girl well." Charlie clenches his jaw stoically. It occurs to me that this is the closest I've ever come to seeing a grown man cry. "We'll get her well. Whatever it takes."

*

Twenty-three years ago, radium was unknown. Today, thanks to constant laboratory work, the power of this most unusual of elements is at your disposal. Through the medium of Undark, radium serves you safely and surely.

After Olive got sick with a bad and lingering flu and Imogen's health continued to go downhill, I went to speak with Miss Harrison and Mr. Weevil. I sat in Mr. Weevil's office – what used to be the principal's office in the old high school – and reported what the Young Doctor had said to me after he'd seen me lip-pointing my brush.

"Two of our girls are very sick right now," I said. "I'm wondering if it might be the radium paint that's making them so ill?"

"Radium making them ill?" Mr. Weevil repeated back at me. He leaned back in his chair and steepled his fingers above his ample belly. "As we all well know, radium is completely safe. Not only that, it is a potent cure-all. It's in all the papers! Perpetual sunshine, they're calling it. And it's all natural! Our paint certainly contains nothing that would make anyone ill. If anything, the radium contained therein makes people stronger and healthier. Wouldn't you agree?"

"If it's in all the papers, I suppose I would, Mr. Weevil."

"May I ask how you yourself are feeling, Miss Morelli?" he asked.

"Why, fine as a daisy, Mr. Weevil."

"And indeed, you are looking quite well," he said. "The very picture of health and youth! Isn't that right, Miss Harrison?"

"She's rosy as a springtime bride, Mr. Weevil," agreed Miss Harrison.

"Some girls are naturally more robust than others," he concluded, with a rap upon his desk. "You're a solid girl. Not small and weak like the others. The other girls are sick simply because they are sickly. Do you understand?"

"I understand," I said. "Thank you kindly, Mr. Weevil."

When I returned to my desk, there were whispers and tears. One of the girls dabbed at her eyes. Carmela explained that Mary Catherine's mother had come to pick her up. She hadn't been feeling well at all and had collapsed on her way out the door.

I looked all around me. Day by day, the other girls were getting paler. Slower. Weaker.

I had honestly never felt better.

*

"Say! Why don't you girls join us for a little petting party?"

We're walking home together on our usual route, only it's later than usual. Darker. It's February so there aren't many sunshine hours. So many girls are off sick these days, we're working extra hours at the plant just to keep up with the demand.

The darker the night, the brighter we glow.

"Mind your potatoes, boys!" says Carmela. Strong and brave and fiery Carmela. She's got a mouth on her, that girl.

She'll swear like a sailor as long as she's not within earshot of St. Columba. But tonight, there is a minor tremor in her voice.

There are three of them. Two big ones and one little one. Not much older than us. Nobody I've seen around town before.

"How 'bout just a little kiss?" One of the big ones grabs a hold of Carmela's wrist. I think about making a break for it to get help, but leaving Carmela alone with all three of them is unthinkable. By then, the other big one has me by both arms.

There's no one else around. No one to call out to. No one to hear us scream.

"Don't you worry 'bout us, lady," says the little one, lifting my skirt. "We're real gentlemen and won't say nothin' to nobody. Scout's honour!"

The bells of St. Columba start chiming. I feel my fingers contract into fists.

If you asked me exactly what happened next, I couldn't tell you. It's like everything dissolved into a gold and green halo of light. The next thing I know, the big one and the little one are on the ground, their faces scraped up and bleeding something awful and I'm watching myself slam them with my fists over and over. When I see that the other big one has Carmela pinned up against the wall, I do to him what I did to the others, kneeing him in the groin for good measure. My fists and knees and elbows are moving faster than my brain can even process. My body does not belong to me.

Not until I reach out for Carmela's hand and we bolt into the night air.

Once we've caught our breaths, Carmela looks at me, incredulous. "Where in the hell did you learn how to do *that?*" Her tone is equal parts amazement and fear.

"I'm not sure, exactly," I say slowly, searching my brain for answers. "I've never actually done it before. But then I thought about wanting to do it and it just happened."

"What you just did," says Carmela. "What I saw back there, sister – that was superhuman."

I don't know how to respond to that. I feel strong. I feel proud. I feel remarkably alive.

Carmela makes the sign of the cross, kisses me on both cheeks and tells me to go get a good night's sleep. There has been far too much excitement for one day.

When I ease into bed next to Allegra, she tells me to turn out the lights. "The lights are already off," I say with a hint of annoyance.

I look down at my fists, still tightly clenched from our terrifying nighttime encounter. They glow a bright and gentle green. Not just the fingertips, as usual, but the entire hand. The entire wrist. Both arms up to the elbow. And beyond the elbow.

I stand to look at myself in the mirror. The top of my head. The tip of my nose. The tops of my feet. I am aglow. It's an internal light, cold yet comforting. It hums a radioactive lullaby to itself. I remove my heavy flannel nightdress and see that the glow is all over. Not just my face and my arms and my toes, but everything in between, too. My ribs and my breasts and my belly. My back and my thighs and my hips and my shoulder blades. All of it. All of me. Undark has enveloped me like a lover.

I stretch out both arms and squint at myself in the darkness and the light. I look as peaceful and powerful as the Madonna, complete with a golden-green halo.

I have become Radium Girl.

I have become pure light.

Acknowledgements

THIS COLLECTION WOULD NOT EXIST WITHOUT THE generous financial support of the Toronto Arts Council, the Ontario Arts Council and the Canada Council for the Arts.

I am profoundly grateful to Samantha Haywood, Paul Vermeersch and Noelle Allen for seeing something in this collection and in me. I am equally grateful to my eagle-eyed and hilarious editor, Jen Sookfong Lee, for "getting it" and pushing me to go deeper. Thank you also to my copy editor, Ashley Hisson, for her unbelievable attention to detail and to Michel Vrana for the gorgeous cover art.

So many fiction writers I admire have touched these pages and helped me along the way – Jessica Westhead, Elyse Friedman, Dennis Bock, Bruce Geddes, Bess Winter, Andrew David MacDonald, Sherwin Tjia, Russell Smith, Suzanne Alyssa Andrew and Ayelet Tsabari – thank you for your generous feedback, your whisky, your wisdom and your friendship. Thank you to Conan Tobias, Daniel Viola, Helen Polychronakos and Leah Golob for publishing my stories and to the Lemon Tree House and Artscape Gibraltar Point for being my creative havens. Thank you to Lindsay Matheson, Valerie Kilgour, Tiffany Sauerbrei, Elizabeth MacLean, Lindsay Lynch, Liisa

Ladouceur, Lucy Cappiello, Katie Franklin and Briony Smith for your enduring friendship, support, hilarity and purest love. Speaking of purest love – Lawrence Jeroen, you are a dream come true and the light at the end of this tunnel. Thank you for all the gifts you have given me. Finally, to my loving and wonderful parents, Steve and Mary Papamarko, thank you for nurturing a deep love of books by reading to us every day and for encouraging me to become a "story writer" when I grew up. And thank you for teaching me to be as caring as you. Empathy is the best possible trait you could have instilled in me – as a writer and as a human being. I am grateful to be your daughter.

Notes

"SOMETHING TO CRY ABOUT"
Nuclear fallout tips taken from:
11 Steps to Survival
Published by the Minister of Supply and Services Canada, 1980
Cat. No. D83-1/4-1980E
ISBN 0-662-11078-1

"RADIUM GIRL"
Italicized information about Undark taken from a 1921 advertisement in *The American Magazine*. https://commons
.wikimedia.org/wiki/File:Undark_(Radium_Girls)
_advertisement,_1921.jpg.

For more information about Undark and the Radium Girls, please see:

Claudia Clark, *Radium Girls: Women and Industrial Health
    Reform, 1910–1935* (Chapel Hill: University of North
    Carolina Press, 1997).
Kate Moore, *The Radium Girls: The Dark Story of America's
    Shining Women* (Naperville, IL: Sourcebooks, 2017).
Sandy Pool, *Undark: An Oratorio* (Madeira Park, BC: Harbour
    Publishing, 2012).

Sofi Papamarko's writing has appeared in the *Toronto Star*, the *Globe and Mail*, the *Montreal Gazette*, *Reader's Digest*, *Chatelaine*, *Flare*, *The Walrus*, the *Huffington Post*, *Exclaim!*, *Salon* and many other publications, both living and dead. Her short fiction has been published in *Taddle Creek*, *Maisonneuve* and *Room*. She lives in Toronto with her partner and his son.